Lonely Is The Night

Julia's Heart is a pebble, shaped by the sea. Her toddler son found it on an Oregon beach and her husband had it engraved with their initials and hung on a chain. It is the one piece of jewelry she never took off, the most identifiable object found with her skeleton, and the thing to which her restless soul is tied.

Julia Lodge was a Black woman married to a white man and raising a small son in Portland, Oregon. Nothing in her fractured memory explains why she's dead, nor how her body wound up in a cave overlooking the sea. Then a teenager stumbles across her remains and the police arrive.

She learns the year is 2018. She's been a missing person since August of 1986. The detective in charge of her case is a racist cop she has a personal history with and the prime suspect is her own beloved husband.

Books by the Same Author

Death and the Redheaded Woman
Death and the Brewmaster's Widow
Death and the Gravedigger's Angel
Death and the Viking's Daughter

Julia's Heart

By

Loretta Ross

ISBN 978-1-7354947-0-8 (trade paperback)
ISBN 978-1-7354947-1-5 (eBook)
ISBN 978-1-7354947-2-2 (audio book)

Cover design by Robin Locke Monda
Cover art by Robin Locke Monda
Book design by Loretta Ross
Whippoorwill Hill Publishing • Missouri USA

Chapter 1

These Dreams

[Heart, 1985]

Julia Lodge woke up dead.

Jude was gone. Julia lay still, listening for the sound of bare little feet on hardwood. Strong light burned red through her eyelids and she curled her arm closer to her stomach, missing the toddler's warmth against her body.

Silence greeted her. No quiet cartoon chatter from the television turned low, no stifled laughter, no scrape of a chair telling her that he was climbing for the cereal.

No cars passing by on the street. No clock ticking quietly on the nightstand. There was an odd musty smell and a faint roar that should not be there; a sound like an approaching storm wind tossing through trees.

Jude was gone.

She put a hand up to shade her eyes and blinked herself awake; sat up slowly and looked around.

She was in a cave.

She had been lying at the edge of a briny pool that covered half the ground surface of a large chamber. Sandy earth sloped upwards behind her and the water lapped towards her feet, wavelets iced with dirty foam. The wall above the water slanted out as it rose, so that the cave was larger at the top than at the bottom. Ten feet up and just left of center a jagged tear in the stone revealed the blazing sun floating in a raggedy patch of blue sky.

Julia looked down at herself. She was dressed for sleep, barefoot and wearing only a long, soft sleep shirt and the necklace she never took off. The sunshine fell across her as a sharply-delineated slash of light. Where it touched, everything glowed with color. Grains of sand sparkled amid the softer, darker earth. The floral pattern on her sleep shirt was bright with pinks and blues and her chestnut skin shone like it was polished. Beyond the reach of the sun, the cavern might have been a study done in charcoal and she a darker shadow against gray stone.

Beside her hand, half-covered with sand and very near to where she'd lain, a human skull stared up at her from eyeless sockets.

Julia gasped and recoiled, scuttling backwards crab-like. A scattering of bones stretched below the skull, towards the water. Pulling herself to her feet, Julia ran around the edge of the pool until she came up against the wall and huddled there, as if it afforded her some protection from whatever phantoms might yet cling to those mortal remains.

In the distance, a motorboat sped by. The Doppler song of its engine invaded the cave, rising in crescendo and then falling away. The water in the pool rippled and splashed.

"Hello?" she called out. "Hello? Can you hear me? Is anybody there? Help! Help me! Help! Hello?"

Her voice fell flat in the dead air and no echoes of her words returned to her. She didn't know where she was. She didn't know how she'd gotten here.

She didn't know where Jude was. He could be lost somewhere in this dark cavern or that vast ocean.

She looked up at the opening in the wall above her head. It was a good ten feet up and narrow, but she had to have come in that way. While some underwater passage obviously connected the pool to the ocean, she couldn't imagine holding her breath long enough to swim it.

The wall was loose dirt over intractable stone. Moist dust and clods of earth formed a heap below the window of sky. Long tan nightcrawlers and tiny white worms writhed and slithered in the dark soil. She moved a few feet to her left, where the slope was more gradual and crawled up it on her hands and knees. The damp mud soaked her nightshirt. She could feel it slippery like a slurry of clay against her skin.

The hole in the cave wall was roughly wedge-shaped, broader at the bottom than at the top, with an uneven floor and small stones poking from the earth on all sides. It was too small for her to pass through. Julia squirmed forward on her stomach, half crawling and half slithering, until she could look out and down. She was halfway up the side of a bluff, above a crescent of dark sand. Beyond, an ocean stretched blue and infinite. Headlands to her left and right cut off this cove from the rest of the shore. The sun hung low, a ball of golden fire on the horizon, closer to the stretch of land on her right than on her left. There was a pile of rubble at the foot of the bluff and, looking up, she could just see the bottom of an un-weathered scar slashing down the rock face. She glanced back into the cave.

Where she was sitting, Julia's body blocked the entirety of the opening. Behind her, the sun threw an unbroken patch of light on the cave floor where she'd awoken and the skeleton that lay there.

———♥———

Julia didn't have amnesia. She didn't know where she was or how she got there. She didn't know what day or even what year it was and she had no memory of any specific thing she'd been doing before ... before ... before whatever had happened to her had happened to her. But she didn't have amnesia.

Characters on TV got amnesia all the time and they'd always announce it by asking, "who am I?" Julia knew exactly who she was.

Her name was Julia Ann (Meyers) Lodge. She was John Lodge's wife, Reuben and Rose Meyers' daughter.

She was Jude's mommy. (Oh, God. Where was Jude?)

She lived, metaphorically speaking, at 1421 Primrose Street, Portland, Oregon, USA. It was a little white bungalow with black trim in a working-class neighborhood south of the river. A blue hydrangea bush grew next to the porch and her fence row, in back, was lined with daffodils. She knew her zip code and her phone number, her birthdate, her social security number, and the license plate numbers of both the family cars.

She knew everything about herself except why she was

dead and how she got that way.

It took her some time and a measure of courage to return to the pool and look more closely at the skeleton. It lay above the high-tide mark, half curled to the right. Its empty eye sockets--Julia's empty eye sockets--looked back at the pool and her hair, her own natural, shoulder-length curls that she had cared for so carefully, were a mess of tangles matted with sand in the rocks below the rise of her forehead. Her teeth had fallen out and her ribs had collapsed to either side and from the pelvis down her bones were half buried in sand and muck. Dark green algae grew on the bones that were showing near the water mark.

———♥———

Daylight waxed and waned in the cave. Julia haunted the opening that afforded her a view of the world. She spent hours (days? Months? Years?) watching the bright and living reality of which she was no longer a part. Consciousness was a fickle thing. She'd awakened with the sun and she'd watched, with a creeping sense of dread and horror, as it set over what had to be the Pacific Ocean. When it rose again it was further south. People appeared on the sand and disappeared as swiftly the moment she blinked or looked away. Boats rode the waves, sometimes for what felt like years. Sometimes they were gone like the echo of a whisper. At night there was a darkness in the reaches of the cave that went beyond simple absence of light.

There was a hollow in her heart where her family's voices should have been, and she kept a running file in her mind of things she wanted to tell them. She'd never realized just how much a part of her they were until now, when they were gone.

She slept sometimes (she supposed it was sleep) and sometimes when she did she dreamed. She dreamt of stormy nights and lightning above the waves and John walking the headlands, calling her name. She tried to remember something. A shopping trip. Tying Jude's shoelaces for him. Making love. Doing laundry. She could remember all these things in the abstract, but she couldn't recall a single specific instance of anything.

She'd avoided venturing too deep into the cave. It wasn't

a simple cavern scooped out of rock. The walls were jagged and uneven, with recesses and crannies that looked like they might run for miles. Julia felt there were other presences there, lurking in the shadows. Wild things. Mad things, or maybe it was only her own madness. Loneliness nestled sharp and bitter in her chest and sang to her in the ringing voice of silence.

She did know that hers weren't the only bones to wind up here. The tide pulled in debris from the ocean constantly--driftwood, and trash and the carcasses of sea creatures. There were the remains of at least two other human bodies here and Julia worried that the insane things in the darkness were a foreshadowing of her own future.

———❤———

One day, when the sun was shining directly in and the light was stronger than usual, she wandered around the edges of the tidal pool. Looking back into the shadows, she caught the edges of a shape that was neither natural nor organic. It was a small tower, bright yellow, with a wider cuff at the bottom and a broken antenna rising from the tip. Julia walked around it, studying it, and found a barely-legible inscription.

"NOAA CASCADE REGION CURRENT PROJECT," it read, and there was a serial number.

"A radio buoy," Julia said to herself, and the words triggered the first hint of a memory. Someone had said something to her about radio buoys. Someone. Someone...

It had been in the summer. She was in an air-conditioned building and she was carrying Jude.

Something about radio buoys, and a barrel. Something about a cat.

It was in a museum. The Seafaring Museum at Waldport, where she and John went every summer to celebrate their anniversary. She could hear the echo of voices in her head. Hers and another. A light voice. Feminine and young. Bright and hopeful and wistful and sad.

Belle. She and Jude had gone to the museum with Belle.

———❤———

Sunlight glinted off the ocean. The movement of the water made the reflection erratic, so that when Julia turned her head, spears of white light found their way around the edges of her sunglasses and made her eyes water. She was carrying Jude on her left hip and she cupped her hand over his face to shield him and hurried up the steps.

Belle was ahead of them, holding the door. Her sunglasses were bigger and her hair was huge, pushed up from her forehead and surrounding her sweet face. Her perm was so fresh, it still smelled faintly of Sulphur. It hadn't escaped Julia's notice how much the younger woman's spiral perm resembled her own natural hair. It was the summer before Belle's sophomore year at Oregon State and she was just beginning to relax into her independence and settle into her own skin. She wore a bright, cotton tee with the sleeves sliced into fringes and a short, ruffled skirt over blue leggings. Long earrings curled down and touched her shoulders and a teardrop-shaped prism hung around her neck on a blue ribbon.

Everywhere she went, she was surrounded by rainbows.

Julia ducked gratefully into the cool, dim interior. Belle followed. The door, closing behind them, cut off the glare and they paused in the foyer, taking off their sunglasses and letting their eyes adjust.

They'd just been to lunch. Julia could still taste crab cakes and hushpuppies. Belle had absentmindedly carried her paper cup in with her. A sharp-faced old man behind a counter to their right gave her a dirty look. She ducked her head apologetically and slurped one last, long drink before dropping it into a nearby trash can. Julia put three dollars in the donation jar and they drifted further into the building.

"This is where the keeper and his family lived." This museum was Belle's idea. She'd been here before and wanted to share it with Julia. "The tower's closed right now for renovation."

The walls were covered with sepia-toned photographs and nautical relics. White ropes protected the exhibits, arrangements of antique furniture and seafaring memorabilia. They stopped beside a barrel made of dark wood, bound with iron. A stand beside it held a typed description and an ancient, over-exposed picture of a freaked-out looking cat.

"The Sarah Jane McGillicuddy," Belle read. "The Sarah Jane McGillicuddy was a triple-masted schooner that plied the lumber trade between San Francisco and Seattle in the late 1870's. On August 14th, 1879, she foundered in a storm off the coast near Waldport. Two crewmembers survived by clinging to the wreckage until they could be rescued the next day, and the ship's cat came ashore unharmed by riding in this barrel. The captain, first mate, and five other crewmen were lost at sea. Their bodies were never recovered."

Julia glanced over her shoulder, out a window and across the bay. It was hard, on such a pretty day, to imagine stormy nights and deadly waters. "I've heard this is a dangerous place to swim," she said. "Though why anyone would want to swim in such cold water is beyond me."

"There's a strong cross current across the mouth of the bay, and an undertow," Belle said. "They almost never recover the bodies of drowning victims. They dropped radio buoys to try to track the current, but they lost the signals."

Jude lay his head on Julia's shoulder, sleepy and content, and fisted his little hand in her neckline between her breasts. One of Belle's rainbows lay on the top of his diaper where it poked up from under his denim shorts.

"I need to refine my major."

Julia cast her a slanted look. "I thought you wanted to talk to dolphins?"

Belle smiled, ducked her head and blushed. The Lodges were fair-skinned, blue-eyed and blonde. "Yeah. I do. But there's so much I could do with oceanography. Some of them are really high-paying jobs, too." She half-pirouetted, letting her fingers trail just above the surface of the picture on the stand. "I was telling my mom about some of the jobs I could get with different degrees, and how much they pay and all."

And that would be what had been bothering her all day. Julia had been waiting. "What did she say?" she prompted.

"She said I should let my husband worry about making money. My job is to keep him happy so that he'll take care of me."

"Your mom's a twat, Belle."

Belle's eyes grew wide and she slapped a hand over her mouth to stifle a shout of laughter. "Aren't you afraid I'll tell her you said that?" she teased.

"Oh, sure. Like you'll say twat."

"I might say it," Belle lied.

"Sure you might."

"I could if I wanted to."

"Then why don't you?" Julia taunted, laughing. "Say it! Say it! Twat. Twat. Say it!"

Belle had her fist in her mouth, giggling helplessly. The old man from the entryway came to the door of the room they were in and gave them a , suspicious look. Belle turned red and nudged Julia with her elbow.

"Hush! He can hear us!"

Julia turned and met the man's eye and he glared and turned away.

"He's a twat too." Jude was slipping and Julia bounced him on her hip, resettling him. His butt felt soggy and she got a whiff of an unpleasant and all-too-familiar odor. "Your nephew needs his diaper changed."

"Oh." Belle glanced around at all the rooms they hadn't visited yet. "We can go."

"Why don't we come back when the tower's open? That's probably the best part."

"Yeah, it probably is. I'm dying to go up and look out the top windows."

As they turned back towards the entrance and the heat of the day beyond, Belle lingered beside the barrel. When she spoke again, her voice was soft and reluctant, as if she were confessing a fault.

"I'm sorry about the sailors," she said, "but I'm glad the cat was okay."

Julia felt a rush of affection. She bumped into Belle, just lightly. A love tap. "Me too, sweetheart," she said. "Me too."

—❤—

While she was lost in the past the light waned. When it was dark and still she slept, if sleep it was, and when the sun returned she roused once more with no clear idea of how much time had gone. Julia always awoke on the sand beside her skeleton, curled on her side as her body had been, looking back into the dark water from whence she must have come. This time she lay there for a long while, thinking about her sister-in-law.

Belle liked to sing and she could carry a tune when she wanted to. She sang pop songs that had more meaning than perhaps even she realized. Girls really do just wanna have fun, and Belle, maybe, more than most. She wore bright colors and long earrings and prisms around her neck and she laughed at stupid jokes and danced with abandon.

When she was around her parents she left off her make-up and jewelry. She tamed her hair into a chaste ponytail and wore long skirts in drab colors and tried so hard to be the daughter they wanted her to be. The Lodges, Muriel especially, were never happy with her.

That was just one of many reasons why Julia didn't get along with her in-laws.

Jude was long-since potty trained and he was too big now for Julia to easily carry him on her hip. The memory was an old one, two or three years probably. But, still, it was a memory. She could add it to the store of things she carried around in her head, rainbows and laughter and fortunate cats to go with the storms and John calling her name.

Julia thought she must be on the coast at Waldport. She didn't recognize this specific stretch of beach, but they visited there regularly so it would make sense. Perhaps they'd gone out in a boat. Maybe they'd gotten caught in a storm and maybe she'd fallen overboard and drowned.

She sighed an insubstantial sigh and rolled over onto her back, away from her bones. The patch of sunlight she lay in was larger than she remembered and when she raised her eyes to the opening in the wall, she found that it had grown. The pile of earth at the base was larger than it had been and sopping mud and she could only guess that a heavy rain had soaked into the ground and caused it to collapse further.

She pulled herself up and picked her way around the new-fallen earth. She could feel the mud and the water and the sand under her bare feet, the heat of the sun and a cold that sometimes made her tremble at night, even though she couldn't lift anything and her fingers slipped through anything she tried to touch. She had wondered how she was able to climb up to the opening, why she didn't just slide through the ground below her and fall forever, but that line of thought made her queasy so she avoided it whenever possible.

She crawled again to the opening, muddy water plastering her nightgown to her body and dripping off her hair. She knew that when she looked down at herself, she would be as clean and dry as she'd been when she started. That didn't make the experience any more pleasant, though.

The top of the passage had fallen as well, so that she had to climb over a mound of mud. Even so it was larger than it had been. For one panic-inducing minute she thought she was stuck, but she wriggled free and slipped out, rolled down the seaward incline and landed in an ungainly heap on the sand.

Chapter Two

I Dream Myself Alive

[A-Ha, 1985]

Julia pulled herself up and looked around. The sand was uncomfortably warm but not hot enough to burn her bare feet. Where she had landed that sand was thinly spread over the darker earth and stone that grew into bluffs behind her. Spurs of land rose to her left and right, but neither reached the water. Outside of the cave, the world was blue and white and golden; water and clouds and sand and sky. The stretch of beach within her view was empty, but voices carried from beyond the bluff to her right. Julia followed them,

Near the high water mark she reached a point from which she could see up and down the coast for a mile or more in each direction. In the next cove to the north there were people. A man in hip boots stood twenty yards out in the ocean, casting a fishing line and reeling it in again and again. A woman lay on a beach towel reading a book while two boys in their early teens chased each other on the sand and tossed a frisbee around. A young German shepherd lolled nearby and a smallish plastic boombox with rounded corners blasted out a song that Julia was unfamiliar with.

Julia approached the woman. She was acutely aware of the fact that she was clad only in a night shirt and she walked gingerly down the beach holding the hem of that shirt down with both hands and rehearsing in her head what she wanted to say.

Please, can you help me? I need to find my family. I have

a husband and a little boy. My husband is John Lodge and my son's name is Jude. My body is in a cave down the beach. I need them to know. I need someone to tell them.

She came up and stopped, standing over the woman. The sun was running low in the sky and the sunbather, holding her book up above her head, cast a misshapen shadow. Nearby sat an open cooler and a bottle of suntan lotion. Each object possessed its own double in the form of a shadowy silhouette on the sand.

Julia alone was unable to make even this most insubstantial mark on the world.

The stranger lay with one knee bent, the other foot stretched out towards the ocean. She was young, with frizzy hair that Julia suspected had been colored once too often and a small roll of fat escaping from her bathing suit bottoms. Her skin was an uncomfortable shade of pink that suggested she hadn't been diligent enough with the sunblock.

Julia waited, breathless, to be noticed. When she was not, she spoke. Only a single word came out and her voice sounded rusty and breathless to her own ears.

"Hello?"

The woman kicked her bent leg out straight, scratched the side of her nose and turned the page on her paperback.

"Hello? Can you hear me? Can you see me? Hello?"

Nothing.

Julia waited out a long few minutes and half a dozen pages turned before she gave up. She looked around and found the dog watching her.

"You can see me," she said. She moved away from the woman, approaching the animal cautiously. His eyes followed her and he crouched low to the sand, tilted his head and flopped his tail in a half-wag. She had the impression that he was not afraid of her, but was wary.

She stopped walking and he rose and circled around, keeping his eyes on her. When he stopped again, she realized he'd placed himself between her and the boys, playing with their frisbee.

"I'm not going to hurt your boys," she said.

The dog sat in front of her and watched her.

She glided forward, stooping and reaching out, desperate for some contact with a living thing. He fell back, with a low sound halfway between a growl and a bark and Julia stopped. She wanted to cry.

"It's okay. I won't hurt you. Don't be afraid. Okay? I'll leave you alone."

A path led up the side of the bluff here and Julia turned that way, hoping to find someone somewhere she could communicate with. Walking away from the small family, she passed close to the tape player. As she did, she felt a quick rush of energy and the music slowed and distorted and died.

For just a few seconds the world around her wavered, like heat rising off an August pavement. The sand shimmered, the waves crackled with energy and the people and the dog blazed in her vision like flames. She was aware of the circle dance of the universe, and of the solar system, and of the molecules that made up the beach and she fell through space as lost and disconnected as a stray electron.

Then she blinked and everything snapped back to normal. Hours, at least, had passed. the people were gone and the dog was gone and the sun was sinking into the horizon. Julia felt as drained as a child coming down from a sugar high. Her eyes drifted closed of their own accord and when she opened them again, she was back in the cave.

━━❤━━

Crawling through the opening the second time was easier. The stretch of beach below Julia's cave was still empty but there were people once more in the next cove to the north. The two expanses of sand looked very much alike to her and she wondered why the one should be shunned. She wondered if perhaps, on some level, people knew about the presence of that dark cavern and the secrets it held.

There were two or three people fishing this time, a gaggle of sunbathers stretched on towels and folding chairs near the water and a beach volleyball game going on. Between the game and the sunbathers, a flock of seagulls had settled in. Julia suspected there'd been a picnic and the birds were cleaning up the crumbs.

The path up to the road lay directly across the beach, with the seagulls in between. None of the people had shown any sign that they'd seen her and she ignored them in turn and headed for the path. She walked through the flock of gulls and they set up a clamorous alarm and exploded away from her into a confusion of feather and wing. Several of the humans nearby stopped to watch their flight, but no one acknowledged Julia or followed her with their eyes.

She climbed up to the level of the road and found it to be a worn blacktop, two lanes separated by fading yellow paint, with a bluff dropping off on the seaward side and dark pines lining it on the east. She looked left and right and then, sharply left again. A hundred yards away the road met another. At the corner sat a squat block building on an empty lot. A shiver of familiarity slipped down her back and she turned towards it, trying to place it. She approached it warily, as someone might draw near to a snake.

She should know this place.

She should *know* this place.

It wasn't until Julia was standing in the cracked and pitted lot, looking straight at the front of the building, that she recognized it. It was empty and deserted now, but in her mind it was bright and busy. It was a little general store called Zoosie's that served homemade ice cream and sold souvenirs to the out-of-towners who came out to the sea every summer. It marked the corner where the road to their vacation cabin left the beach access road and every time they came up from Portland they'd stop there first for ice cream floats.

She wondered when it had gone out of business. Not recently, that was certain. The sign that had stood out front was gone, nothing now but a broken, rusty pole. Weeds poked through cracks in the asphalt parking lot and the gas pumps were gone. Only pipes rising up from a concrete island remained to testify to their existence.

Julia drifted close to the building and was surprised to see dark eyes watching her from behind the dusty glass of the window in the front door. She circled the entrance. The figure didn't move but it seemed to her the eyes followed her. Hopeful and unnerved, she closed the distance. It wasn't until she was nearly touching the glass that she realized she was looking at a picture.

A familiar picture.

She leaned in and put her hands up to shield her eyes, blocking the daylight to help herself look beyond the dusty glass. A poster, fading and ripped at one corner, was still taped to the inside of the door. Julia's own face looked back at her. Above the picture was a single word, printed in block letters.

MISSING

Chapter Three

So Far Away

[Dire Straits, 1985]

"Why are you wearing your nightgown?"

Julia turned around slowly. She was standing against a sagging wire fence, looking at the back of the one building in Waldport that she knew and knew well. It was a little, white clapboard vacation cottage, set off by itself at the end of a row of like cottages.

A little girl stood on the sand behind her, looking at her curiously.

"You can see me?"

The child shrugged, an elaborate gesture that involved raising her shoulders, tilting her head and twisting her hands to show Julia her palms. "Yeah, sure. Why are you in your nightgown?"

"I don't know. I'm lost. I'm trying to find my family."

"Where did you see them last?"

"I don't know. Maybe here."

Under her picture, the poster had said, "MISSING from Waldport, OR, August 7, 1986. AGE: 28. SEX: Female. Height: 5'5". WEIGHT: 133 lbs."

That was all. But if she'd been in Waldport before she went missing, she'd have been here.

"This is where my family is staying." The child came up to stand at the fence beside Julia and look at the cottage. It wasn't a fancy place. White paint flaked off the siding and rusty splotches covered the screen wire over the windows. The back yard was mostly bare earth. The fence that separated it from the beach was made of sagging field fence strung between twisted, weathered wooden posts. Weeds and wildflowers grew around and through the wire. "I'm Emma Grace."

Emma Grace was no more than seven. She was a thin child, with long dark hair and big dark eyes. A bright, neon pink barrette was slipping out of her hair and there was a streak of dirt beside her nose. Her arms and legs were dusty and her feet were bare. She was filthy, the way only a busy child can be, but her clothes under the dust and sand were bright and good quality.

"I'm Julia. It's nice to meet you. It's been a long time since I had anyone I could talk to."

Emma tipped her head and looked up at Julia curiously. "You have a string on your back."

"Do I?"

"Yeah. A long, shiny string. It's stretched out that way." She pointed back up the beach, towards the cave. "It looks like it's tied to you."

"Oh. Maybe it is. I tried to walk back to Portland, but I could only go so far before something pulled me back."

"Portland's a long way."

"Yes, I know. But I want to go home."

Emma stood on tiptoe and batted at something behind Julia's back.

"I can't touch it." She poked one finger delicately at Julia and watched it disappear into her arm. "Are you a ghost?"

"I think I must be. But I'm not going to hurt you. Don't be afraid."

"I'm not. I always wanted to see a ghost. My whole life."

"Goodness. Your whole life?"

Emma Grace nodded earnestly. "Do you haunt the house or the beach?"

"Both, I guess. This is where we stay when we come here in the summer. John and I spent our honeymoon here and every summer we spend a week here for our anniversary."

"Is John your husband?"

"Yes. And we have a little boy named Jude. Well, Julian, but we call him Jude."

Experience had shown Julia that she could go about 500 yards from the cave before something dragged her back. This cottage was at the southern end of her range and as she moved away from Emma Grace, toward the corner of the fence, she could feel something tightening and dragging on her between her shoulder blades.

"I remember..."

"Remember what?"

"Being here. With Jude, late in the afternoon. There's a parking area in front of this cottage, right? A big circle where people leave their cars to go down to the beach. It's where the road ends, except for a driveway that goes up to the house on the hill."

"Where the weird old people live."

"They're not weird. They're just a little different. They're nice, though. We were talking to Charlie. Mr. Miller. We were standing by the gate to his driveway. He was sick."

———♥———

"*Thank you for showing us the way back.* I'm sorry we were trespassing. I didn't realize we'd gotten so far off the road."

She had a plastic bowl full of blackberries in her left hand and she was holding onto Jude with her right. His little fist was sticky and there were berry stains around his mouth.

"Don't worry about that," Charlie Miller said. He was probably only in his forties but he looked much older. A dirty red bandana was tied loosely over his bald head and he wore tattered blue jeans and a drab green tee shirt. In spite of the late summer heat, a jean jacket hung from his thin shoulders. The skin of his face sagged and his cheekbones showed sharply.

"I just don't want either of you to get hurt. It's a long way to the hospital if you get bit."

He was leaning on a cane, trying to be nonchalant about it, but it was obvious he was barely able to stand. His face and neck were burned a deep red and his complexion, under the burn, was pale and waxy. There was a single car in the parking area, an old red Chrysler, and Charlie glanced toward the beach, his shoulders tense and his eyes narrowed. Julia followed his gaze and saw a strange man pacing the sand with a metal detector.

"You're not staying here alone?"

"Just for tonight. John will be here tomorrow evening."

"All right, then. You just holler if you need anything."

———♥———

"It was just Jude and I. John wasn't with us. But I don't remember ever coming down with just Jude. Why would we have come alone? Where was John?"

After spending so much time alone, Julia had become accustomed to speaking aloud. She didn't even realize she was doing it until Emma Grace answered her.

"I dunno. Where would he be?"

"I don't know either."

"You say that a lot."

"I know. I don't know much of anything, it seems."

"Emma Grace!"

They turned together at the shout coming from the back of the cottage. The door had opened and a plump woman with bleach-blonde hair was leaning out. "Emma Grace! Come in now. It's time for supper."

"Mom! Come meet Julia! She's a ghost."

The woman came out and strolled across the yard. "Hello, Julia."

Julia stood up straight, shocked, and smoothed her sleep shirt down over her thighs.

"You can see me?"

Emma Grace's mother leaned down and patted an imaginary head and Julia drooped.

"She's not a little kid, Mom," Emma Grace said, her voice dry. "You almost touched her butt, though."

"Well, I'm sorry. She's just going to have to excuse you. Dinner's ready."

"Can I come back out and talk to her some more after dinner?"

"I don't think so. Early bed time tonight. We're heading home tomorrow and we need to get up and get ready first thing."

"But I don't want to," the child whined.

"I didn't ask you," her mother whined back. "C'mon. House. Now."

Pouting, Emma Grace went around through the gate and followed her mother to the house.

"Emma Grace, wait!" Julia called. "Where's home?"

Emma Grace turned, walking backward as she talked. "Portland."

"And do you go to school there?"

"Yeah."

"When you go back this autumn, will you watch for my son? Jude, remember? I don't know how old he might be now, but I think he might be in school. His name is Julian, but we call him Jude. Please, watch for him? And if you see him? Tell him I love him."

Chapter Four

Don't You (Forget About Me)

[Simple Minds, 1985]

The teenage boy who found Julia's skeleton was singing opera. The opening had grown enough that late afternoon sunlight leaked in around him when he stuck his head in and he was able to see the extent of the cave beyond just a hole in the bluff.

He pulled himself in headfirst, then swiveled on his butt at the entrance and slipped down to the cavern floor.

"Hello? Hellooo-ooo?" He was maybe thirteen, a thin-faced boy with brown hair sticking up at the back and freckles across his nose. After testing the acoustics he launched into an enthusiastic barrage of Figaros. He was developing a nice baritone, but it regressed to a pre-pubescent tenor when he realized the white object shining in the patch of light was a human skull.

He froze and swallowed several times. His breathing was ragged and he backed to the wall as if he didn't dare turn his back on Julia's bones. At the last minute he turned away, clawed his way up to the opening and was gone.

He returned, before the light was completely faded, in the company of a young man in a Lincoln County Sheriff's Department uniform.

"...and then I looked down, and he was just lying there."

"He's a skeleton," the cop said. "What were you expecting him to do?"

"Not be there?"

"Okay, I'll give you that one."

Julia moved back and down, away from the entrance. The deputy didn't come all the way in, but lay in the passage and shined a flashlight around the cave.

"So what do you think?" the kid asked.

"I think you found a body."

"Pretty cool, huh?"

"Yeah, I wouldn't lead with that on your OK Cupid profile."

He moved away and Julia could hear him talking cop talk over a radio. She settled on the sand beside her remains and waited and worried.

Other people started showing up right away. One by one they crawled into the entrance and shone flashlights down on her skull, moved their lights around the cavern, then left again. By the time someone else actually entered the cave the sun had left it. The first people to come in, eerie figures in white clothing reminiscent of surgical scrubs, started out by stringing electrical cables and setting up spotlights. The bright white lights cast sharp shadows and threw the people's faces into relief, distorting their appearances so that they seemed barely human.

One man--or woman, Julia couldn't tell. One person was taking pictures with a small box about the size of Julia's pocketbook.

"What is that? Seriously. That can't be a camera. Is that a toy?"

No one answered her. She'd become accustomed, in her dealing with beachgoers, to being ignored. It seemed a little more personal when they were standing over her body, though.

A second investigator used a tape measure to measure everything in the cavern and then sat down in the sand, well away from her skeleton, to sketch a diagram. Three men came in last. One, she realized after a minute, was the young deputy who'd been first on scene. The other two were strangers. One was tall and broad-shouldered, the other smaller and softer and rounder, but they both carried themselves with the air of people who were used to being in charge. Julia noted the subtle ways the others in the cavern deferred to them: moving back, looking busy, turning a little to keep from having their back to the pair.

"There's a high tide mark," the young deputy said. "That pool is connected to the ocean. Drowning victim, you think?"

"That's the most likely explanation," the smaller man said. He wore a name tag that identified him as Dalton, a medical examiner stationed at Clackamas. "We'll know more after the autopsy."

"Have we lost anyone recently? I don't remember any drowning deaths in the last few years. Not here."

They were looking her skeleton over but not touching her yet.

"It's not recent." The tall man finally spoke and some quality of his voice, echoing in the dark chamber, sent a shiver up her spine. He pointed out the scum and algae growing over the bones of her feet and lower legs. "And it's not a he, unless I miss my guess."

"No. No, look at the shape of that pelvis. This is a woman. A Black woman, I'd bet, just on what I've seen so far."

"How can you tell?" The young deputy asked.

"The shape of her eye sockets. More rectangular than rounded, usually indicates African heritage. Her nasal cavity is wider and the bridge of her nose less pronounced than you'd expect in a Caucasian skull."

The larger man moved up beside her head and went down to one knee. "We get all the pictures we need?"

"So far," said the figure with the camera.

"Okay, don't go anywhere." He brushed aside the sand and dirt around her shoulder blade and her upper ribs. In the harsh light of the spotlight Julia could see that he was an older man, middle aged at least. His eyebrows were nearly completely gray and there were tension lines on his forehead and at the corner of his eyes. His fingers stilled and he smiled an unpleasant, predatory smile.

"Get a shot of this in situ."

"What have you got?" Dalton asked.

The man waited until his colleague had taken a series of photos of his find, then picked up an object from the sand between her ribs, brushed it off and held it up. It was a heart-shaped stone, drilled and strung on the remains of a gold chain. Julia didn't have to see it up close to know that it was engraved with a trio of interlocking J's.

John. Jude. Julia.

Jude had found the stone on the beach at Waldport the year he was three and John had had it made into a pendant for her. It had been a Christmas gift to her from the two of them.

The senior cop turned it in his hand and looked at it.

"Hello, Julia," he said. "I've been looking for you for a long time."

It was her name on his lips that triggered the memory.

———♥———

The jail cell smelled like disinfectant. It was strong but not entirely effective, because under that stench lingered the remains of stale beer, urine, and vomit. Julia sat gingerly on the edge of the cot, not trusting the mattress to be anything approaching clean. She was wearing a cute pair of white short-shorts and a midriff-baring purple top with ruffles at the shoulders. Her hair was still almost perfect from her wedding that morning but hot, angry tears had washed most of her makeup away.

The outer door opened and she looked up. Her jaw ached from clenching it. The young deputy who'd arrested her unlocked her cell and waved for her to follow him.

"Where are you taking me?" she demanded.

"You're free to go," he said. He wasn't meeting her eyes. His mouth tightened as if he'd eaten something sour. "Your husband's here."

Julia jumped up and pushed past him, out of the holding area and down the hall to the small lobby just inside the exit door. John was waiting for her. His back was a little straighter than it really needed to be. His face was hard, his eyes narrowed, and as she came through the door he took her hand and pulled her protectively against his side.

He turned on the cop.

"Aren't you even going to apologize?"

"I never apologize for doing my job."

"Doing your job? Doing your *job*?"

"Law officers have to use our judgement to figure out what's going on in any given situation. I may have been wrong this time, but 99 times out of 100 I'm going to be right."

Julia turned on him. "I want your name and badge number."

The cop sighed and rolled his eyes.

"Donaldson," he said. "My name is Deputy Manfred--"

———♥———

"Donaldson!"

The cop holding Julia's pendant turned at the shout. There was a figure silhouetted in the entrance waving a glowing square.

"Sheriff wants an update."

"Tell him I'll call him back."

"But..." the figure hesitated. "...okay."

Julia stared at Donaldson.

"I know you. I *know* you, you sonofabitch! But...you were my age?"

Donaldson turned back to the coroner. "I think you're going to find that she didn't drown."

"I think you're right," the other man said drily. He held up Julia's skull and tipped it gently to the side.

There was a neat, round hole just above the point where her spine would have attached.

"Sift that sand carefully," the coroner advised. "You're looking for a bullet."

Chapter Five

I Know What I Know

[Paul Simon, 1986]

They loaded her bones into a body bag, packed up her skull in a box and took her back to the state medical examiner's lab. There were no seats in the back of the coroner's wagon so she perched on the end of the stretcher and hoped she wasn't sitting on herself.

Donaldson followed in an oversized wagon-thing. It was a big, dark red teardrop that looked like it should be the emergency escape pod in a spaceship. As they approached the point on the highway where she'd been dragged back before she braced herself, in case it was the cave that had a hold on her, rather than her bones. She felt no pull in the middle of her back this time, though. They spun past the boundary without incident, hit the highway and turned towards Clackamas.

Her mind teemed with questions she had no one to answer. What year was this? How long had she been gone? Where was her family now?

More than half of the cars were some version of a cross between a Ford Bronco and a small passenger van. They were passed by one low-set sports car, riding barely above the pavement, and a powerful bass beat shivered through the vehicle she was riding in. There were buildings she didn't remember along the highway and billboards that were giant televisions. Even the normal billboards were nonsensical, saying things like "like us on Facebook" or "follow us on Twitter".

When the cops had carried the stretcher with her remains across the beach, almost everyone in the gathered crowd had been chattering away on transistor radios, or holding them up and pointing them at the police procession.

They reached the medical examiner's office and drove around the building. The lot was almost empty under bright security lights. At the back of the building, they stopped in front of a closed garage door and Dalton got out of the van and walked back. He took a credit card from his wallet and slid it through a channel next to a keypad, then punched in a series of numbers. The door slid up.

"Well," Julia said, "isn't that just skip diggity?"

They slid the gurney with her skeleton out of the van and wheeled her down a hall and into a large room. One wall was covered with drawers and there were three free-standing tables with drainage systems and a collection of rolling carts stocked with shiny equipment. Microphones hung from the ceiling over each table and there were televisions up in the corners of the room.

"I'm not going to start on her tonight," the M.E. told Donaldson.

"Could you just lay out the bones a little? Make them look like a skeleton?"

"Why?"

"Her family is on the way. Her mother should be here any time now. Her husband and son will be along in a little while."

"They're coming here? Now?" Julia clenched her fists and looked towards the door, as if she could see them through the wood.

Dalton's reaction was less enthusiastic.

"Shit, Donaldson. You notified them? I haven't even verified her identity."

"It's her."

"Yeah, probably. But, still."

"Anyway, I didn't notify anybody. Word about the body leaked and they called me."

"You couldn't tactfully tell them to stay home and wait for us to know something?"

Donaldson snorted. "You tell Rose Meyers what she can

and can't do. I'll watch. Besides, I want to know how her husband reacts when he sees the body."

"You think he killed her?"

"What?" Julia turned on Donaldson. "That's crazy!"

"Oh, yeah. I'm damned sure he did. And now that I finally have a body, maybe I can prove it."

"That's insane," she said again. "It's the stupidest thing I've ever heard. He'd never hurt anyone, least of all me or Jude. And no one who actually knows us could ever even dream of such a thing."

Donaldson's pocket played a snippet of hard rock music. He pulled out the little, black device that she'd been assuming was a transistor radio, ran one finger across the glowing screen and put it up to his hear. "Donaldson." He listened for a minute. "Okay, bring her in."

He touched the screen again and dropped it back in his pocket.

"Julia's mother is here."

———♥———

Age had shrunken Rose Meyers. She was a good three or four inches shorter than she had been when Julia had last seen her, but her posture was still ramrod straight. The skin of her face and hands was papery, covered with fine wrinkles across her fingers and around her mouth. Her hair was completely white now, her hair and her eyebrows, fine as dandelion down against her dark skin. She smelled of lavender perfume and Dial soap with a stringent undertone of BenGay and Absorbine Jr.

A female deputy showed her into the room, a stout South Korean woman with a delicate face and the build of a bouncer.

"Where's my daughter?"

Dalton stepped up quickly. "Ma'am, we haven't confirmed the decedent's identity yet."

Rose ignored him, focusing on Donaldson.

"We just got here," he said. "She still in this body bag. Do you really want to see? It's just bones."

"Show me."

He unzipped the bag, then picked up the box with her skull and took it out, setting it at the end of the table.

"It's her," she said with certainty.

"Probably," he agreed. "We'll have to compare dental records to be sure. I found this under the body though." He produced Julia's heart necklace, sealed in an evidence bag with its caked and corroded chain.

Rose's mouth tightened. "That's Julia's," she said. "She never took it off. It's her." She did not give in to tears but was tense, her voice hard with anger. "Did you arrest that bastard John Lodge yet?"

"Mama!" Julia exclaimed. "What are you saying?"

"Not yet." Donaldson tucked the bag with the necklace back into his pocket. "But I have a real chance, now that we have some evidence to work with. I promised you once and I'll tell you again. I'm going to nail him for this."

"How did she die?"

Donaldson opened his mouth but the M.E. beat him to it.

"We can't say yet. We're going to need to do an autopsy. We'll let you know when we know something."

Rose nodded.

"And they found her where, again?"

"In a cave. It was connected to the sea by a subterranean passage. The killer must have dumped her body in the ocean, outside the cove, and it washed into the cave through the passage. A landslide opened the cave to the outside and a teenager went in poking around and found her. The person who dumped her body would have to have been someone who understood the tides and the currents in the area."

"They vacationed there every year since they got married. John would have known. And Belle was studying oceanography. She'd have known."

"Where is Belle?" Julia asked. "Is she coming too?" Like all her questions, it went unanswered.

"That would explain a lot," Donaldson agreed.

A normal wall telephone rang and Dalton answered it. He put his hand over the mouthpiece and turned back to speak to Donaldson. "The Lodges are here."

"Oh, thank God." Julia wanted to see them so badly it hurt.

"I'll just be going then," Rose said. "I have no desire to see that son of a bitch right now. Tell my grandson to call me."

"Of course." Donaldson turned to the coroner. "Dalton, can you show Mrs. Meyers out the back way so she can avoid our other guests?"

Dalton gave him a dirty look but acquiesced. When they were gone from the room, the senior cop turned to the younger woman.

"John Lodge and I have a history, so I'm going to go. I want to know how he reacts without me around to put on a performance for. I want you to stay here. Act nice. Sweet and sympathetic. I want to know everything he says and everything he does. When you come back, bring me the security tapes. Use your feminine wiles." He gave her a critical look. "If you have any. Try not to screw up."

He left the lab. Just before the door closed she saw him turn left, towards the garage and the way they'd come in. When he was gone the female deputy relaxed. Her nametag said Min and she couldn't have been more than twenty-four. She went over to the table to look at Julia's remains and spoke aloud to her.

"Miss Julia, I am awfully sorry about whatever happened to you. I gotta tell you, though. If you have to be in the room with Donaldson, dead is probably the way to go."

Julia laughed, surprised. "I'm going to assume he's still an asshole?"

Somewhere in the empty building a door clanged and she could hear voices. They were too faint for her to understand the words, but she knew the tone, knew the cadence of his speech.

She turned to face the door, tense, her right hand fisted at her breast. She could hear at least three sets of footsteps approaching down the hall. One of them was John's and one would have to be Jude's, all grown up now.

They grew louder. The doorknob began to turn.

And then there was a sudden tug at her back, a quick rush of pressure and she was flying backwards, through steel and concrete block. The force, or string, or whatever it was that was tying her down had snapped back and it pulled her through the Oregon night, through pools of darkness and slashes of light until she fell through the closed door of a car and found herself sitting in the front seat of a moving vehicle.

The figure to her left was a dark silhouette until they passed a streetlight and a band of illumination showed her his profile.

It was Donaldson.

Chapter Six

In The Shape Of A Heart

[Jackson Browne, 1986]

Donaldson returned to Waldport, Julia his unwilling passenger. He drove without music, chewing on his upper lip and tapping out random patterns on the steering wheel with his thumbs.

Only the chatter from his police band radio broke the silence. It was all mundane. Apparently, whatever had needed to be said about Julia's body had already been said. There was a fight in a convenience store parking lot and a shoplifter at Walmart. The manager of a fast food restaurant needed an escort to the bank and someone complained about a barking dog.

At Newport he went through the drive thru of a Taco Bell and had to wait nearly fifteen minutes for a bag of tacos and a soda pop. The fast food restaurant was almost unrecognizable, its familiar brown, yellow, and orange color scheme overtaken by cream and charcoal. T-shirts and baseball caps had replaced the heavy polyester uniforms and visors. The menu was huge and, to Julia's eye, the prices were exorbitant.

She had half expected him to return to the cave but instead he drove to the sheriff's department and spent the next odd hour or so setting up a folding table in the corner of his office and organizing sealed cartons another deputy had brought over from long-term storage.

What they contained, Julia couldn't imagine. She read the labels on a few but all she could make out was a case number, Donaldson's name, and a range of dates in the spring and summer of 1987.

So much had changed in this world, but the clock on the wall was still just a clock and when the hour hand touched midnight he turned off his office light, closed his door and left. There were a couple of deputies working at desks in the squad room as he passed through but he didn't stop to say goodbye and neither of them looked up to wish him goodnight.

He pulled up in front of a plain, ranch-style house in a quiet residential neighborhood. The surrounding houses were mostly dark, with just a few odd windows flickering from the light of television sets. Music was playing somewhere, too soft and too far away to identify, and the air smelled like rain.

Donaldson unlocked the house, then paused to pull his mail from the mailbox and pick up a folded newspaper from the porch floor. Julia slipped past him and hovered inside the door, a reluctant and unwelcome guest. He flipped on the light and she looked around while he emptied his pockets on a table by the door.

Someone had put thought into the living room. A pair of armchairs with heavy wood frames coordinated with a long, low coffee table and a telephone stand. The chair cushions were upholstered with a floral print in shades of teal green and pale gold, colors echoed in the drapes at the window and the large throw rug in the center of the hardwood floor. But sunlight had faded the drapes; the fabric was darker and brighter in the pleats at the edge of the tieback. A corner of the nearest chair seat had begun to fray and an entertainment center that matched the rest of the pieces had been shoved into a corner, where it served as a catchall.

The sofa was new, a decadent affair in deep brown leather that neither complimented nor clashed with the rest of the furniture. It occupied the center of the room, facing a wall that was entirely taken up by a huge screen.

Fascinated, Julia went over to study it more closely.

"Is this your television?"

The biggest TV she'd ever seen had been a massive 36-inch affair in the window of an electronics shop at the mall. It had been a projection television, basically just a large screen with a small device below and in front of it to receive and transmit the picture. The price tag had been well over $2,000 and the picture on it was hard to see in the brightly-lit mall.

This television, if television it was, dwarfed that one. Julia had always understood that TVs larger than about 26 inches were impracticable because the massive picture tubes required would make them far too heavy and bulky. But here was this screen, mounted on the wall. Wondering if it were somehow set into the structure of the house, she peeked. It truly was only three or four inches thick with nothing in the space behind it but a tangle of cables and a cobweb jungle.

Two of the cables led to black boxes on a cheap-looking bookshelf wedged between the edge of the screen and the adjoining wall. One of them she guessed to be a cable box and the other some 21st century iteration of a VCR. There wasn't a VHS tape in sight but the bookshelf was crammed full of slender plastic cases and she recognized some of the names on the spines as movie titles.

"So many Star Wars movies! There are four Indiana Jones films now? I loved those. I was going to dress Jude as Indiana for that next Halloween. I found a toy whip at a flea market and John bought him a leather jacket. We were still looking for a little fedora."

She traced her fingers idly across the rows. Donaldson had taken a seat on the sofa behind her and she could hear him rustling the paper.

"The last movie I went to was a Disney film. The Great Mouse Detective. Belle and I took Jude to a matinee while John was working. The last movie John and I saw together was a comedy called Short Circuit. It was about a robot that got struck by lightning and became conscious. 'Johnny Five is alive.' Unlike me..." Her voice caught in her throat. She grasped the edge of the shelf for support and turned her head to look at Donaldson. She felt as if he should be able to hear her, should be conscious of her presence somehow. But of course he was not.

She went back to the movies, forcing her attention away from her own plight.

"There was one coming out that John wanted to see.

Stand By Me, I think? We talked about seeing it while we were on vacation. I just now remembered that. And there was another Star Trek coming out at Christmas time. Belle was excited about that one. It was going to have whales."

She turned her back on the shelf and leaned against it, crossing her arms over her chest. She was cold suddenly for no real reason.

"No one mentioned where Belle was today. She didn't come with John and Jude? I wonder where she is now? I hope it's someplace wonderful. I hope she's on a scientific expedition, on a ship in the south Pacific. Hell, by now maybe she's leading a scientific expedition."

She tried to imagine her sister in-law middle-aged. She'd be beautiful still, Julia thought. Lean and tanned and quietly confident. She pictured her surrounded by rapt students. An assistant in the background. "Dr. Lodge! Dr. Lodge! National Geographic is on the phone again. They want to do another cover story about you."

"This isn't fair, you know," Julia said, looking at Donaldson. He was cutting something out of the sports pages with a pocket knife, careless of the coffee table under it. "I shouldn't be here, trapped in your living room, wondering what's become of my family."

Her heart hurt. A few tears escaped, ran down her cheeks and disappeared before they hit the floor. Donaldson pulled himself up, took his trash to the kitchen and returned with a beer.

He went to the shelf full of movies and chose something in a plain, battered case.

"You're going to watch a movie? Oh, this should be interesting."

The case yielded a disc that looked like a CD. He slid it halfway into the smaller black box, dropped onto the sofa, and turned the TV on with a remote that he dug out of the cushions. The first thing that came up, with shocking clarity, was a colorful moving graphic. The black box made a whirring, clunking noise. It pulled the disk the rest of the way in and the graphic gave way to what appeared to be vintage newsreel footage of battle. Anti aircraft guns fired and recoiled.

"A war movie," Julia said. "Not what I'd have chosen but okay." She settled herself in the nearest chair and leaned forward, prepared to be entertained.

"Germany," a male voice announced. "Nineteen-forty-three. The country is at war. The world is in chaos. But even in the midst of chaos there must be someone to maintain order."

The newsreel footage disappeared and was replaced with a sultry blonde female in a peaked cap and Nazi dominatrix apparel standing against a red background. Beside her jagged black broken Gothic letters read:

STERN NURSE NAN AND THE NAUGHTY UNDER-FUHRER

Julia scrambled up. "Oh, hell no."

A muscular young blond man appeared on screen wearing a German officer's coat and cap and a pair of tightie whities. His hands were bound in front and his eyes downcast. He raised his head and gave the camera a sultry look.

"Ich bin ein bad boy."

Julia fled for the dark kitchen, followed by a zipper sound she suspected did not come from the television.

———♥———

Later that night, much later, after Donaldson had turned off the TV and gone to bed, Julia wandered the dark house. There was more to see out the French doors in the kitchen, but something kept drawing her back to the living room and the window by the front door. She followed the wall as much as she could, giving the sofa—and the soggy sock abandoned on the floor in front of it—a wide berth.

It was raining again, a soft, gentle drizzle. Raindrops meandered down the windowpane, casting translucent shadows across the patch of yellow light that came in from the street and lay across the table by the door. Watching those shadows, Julia realized there was something familiar among the detritus Donaldson had emptied from his pockets.

It was the not-quite-perfect outline of a stone heart,

sealed in a plastic evidence bag. When Donaldson had left the morgue that day he'd taken with him her last tangible connection to her husband and son.

Chapter Seven

One Moment In Time

[Whitney Houston, 1988]

"I was told they found more bodies?"

The sheriff was young. He wore a tailored uniform and an expensive watch and his office was decorated with pictures of himself at civic events. He greeted Donaldson deferentially. "Our friends with the press are going to want to know what we can tell them."

Donaldson helped himself to a seat in front of his boss' desk. "They've found remains from at least four more individuals. It's going to take some time to identify them. None of them are anywhere near as complete as Julia Lodge's skeleton is."

"Do we have a serial killer on our hands?"

"That's unlikely. Dalton thinks the other remains are a lot older. Some of them maybe as much as a hundred years or more. Most likely drowning victims. Swimming accidents, shipwreck, that sort of thing. It's going to take months to process them. For now, I figured we'd make Lodge our priority, since we have hard evidence of foul play."

"She was shot?"

Donaldson hesitated. "We...think so."

"You don't know?"

"The damage to the skull looks like a bullet hole to the naked eye, but we haven't found the slug. There was no exit wound, so it should still be there."

"Could it have washed away?"

"Her teeth didn't. Her head was just above the high-water mark. I don't know. We're going to keep looking. We'll know more once Dalton has finished his autopsy, but it could take weeks to get all the tests back."

"So what do I tell the paper?"

Donaldson's mouth tightened and the corner of his left eye twitched. He turned his head to the left for a second, then slid forward in his chair, put his arms on the sheriff's desk and looked the sheriff in the eye.

"You know, sir, I've been around a long time. I actually remember Julia Lodge. Tell them that. I *knew* her. She was a very special lady. And I am not going to stop until I've learned the truth, and we are in a position to give her the justice that her soul has been crying out for for more than three decades now."

"Excellent," the sheriff beamed. "Excellent! And I'll give you whatever I can to make that possible."

"Great." Donaldson rose. "Can I have Oliver and Min?"

"Sure. Um...I'll need them to make some patrols though. We're still short-handed."

"Of course. Whenever they're available."

"Whenever we can cut them free, they're all yours." The sheriff rose as well, shook Donaldson's hand and walked him to the door of his office. Julia slipped out as soon as that door was opened and followed the senior deputy across the squad room.

Donaldson snapped his fingers and singled out the young deputy who'd been first to respond at the cave and the woman who'd been at the medical examiner's office.

"Oliver, Min, you're with me until further notice."

The two rose and, along with Julia, followed him into his office. Donaldson held the door for them, slamming it behind himself and dropping into the swivel chair behind the single desk. He pulled a stack of files over to the center of the desk, folded his hands on top of them, and grinned at his subordinates.

"You seem happy," the male deputy--Oliver?--observed suspiciously.

"I. Am. Delighted." He took an 8x10 of Julia from the top file and slapped it down on the wood. "After thirty years, I'm going to nail John Lodge for killing this bitch."

————❤————

"Tani-something. Mura, I think. Tanimura. Yeah. That was it."

Julia hovered uncomfortably just inside the door of room 127 in River Walk Assisted Living Facility and looked around. Things had changed since the last time she'd visited someone in a nursing home. The television was another big, flat panel, bolted to the wall, with a picture quality so vivid it was surreal. That seemed to be the norm now. It was showing Jeopardy, staged on an unfamiliar set and hosted by a suddenly white-haired and venerable Alex Trebek.

The halls that had brought them here were long and narrow, lined with carts and potted plants and elderly people parked in wheelchairs, staring at nothing. It smelled like strong, artificial floral perfume with underlying hints of antiseptic and industrial cooking.

"Who?" Donaldson asked.

"Tanimura." The elderly lady they had come to talk to was ensconced in a little, square vinyl recliner. She had an oxygen tank tucked in beside her. The mask rested on her lap.

Min waited near the window, notebook and pen at the ready. Donaldson paced. He caught Min's eye and made a minute twirling motion towards his head. The old lady saw as well.

"I am not crazy," she said shortly. "I'm telling you what I remember. I had rented that cottage to a family named Tanimura."

"Mrs. Garrity?" Julia asked, moving further into the room so she could see her better. She remembered the woman who had owned the vacation cottages as a middle-aged sprite. She was small and thin, with curly brown hair and blue eyes bright behind oversized glasses. Julia had never seen her without an open can of Pepsi and a lit cigarette. She'd also never seen her sit still before.

"They were Asian, I think. The Tanimuras. Anyway, they rented that cottage the first week of August. But their youngest daughter--maybe it was a son. A kid. Their youngest kid got appendicitis. Had to go back to Salem and put it in the hospital. Weren't going to be able to come back. The place was paid up and just sitting there empty. No sense in it sitting there empty. And the Lodges, they were regulars. So I called them and I offered to let them come down a few days early."

Now her hair was stark white, straight and short, like a schoolboy would have worn in the fifties. Her skin, tanned to a dull dark brown, stretched taut across her cheekbones. Her cheeks were sunken and her mouth was ringed all around by tiny lines

"Did you know them well?" Min asked.

"The Lodges, not the Tanimuras," Donaldson clarified.

Mrs. Garrity lifted the mask in one gnarled hand and put it over her mouth and nose. She shot Donaldson an irritated frown over the clear plastic and took three or four breaths before lowering it and speaking again.

"I don't know. Sorta well. I thought I did. As well as I knew any of my regulars. Cute couple. They spent their honeymoon here, which I think *you* know." That was directed at Donaldson. "Came here every year after for their anniversary. Every year until she went missing. Brought their little boy. Jude. I remember Jude. Cute kid. John Lodge's little sister would come down sometimes too. Just for a day or two, babysit the kid."

"You called them at home? In Portland, right?"

"Did they live in Portland?"

"Yes."

"Then I probably called them in Portland."

Donaldson sighed. "Okay, so you called them up and offered them the cabin for a couple of extra days. Who did you talk to, do you remember? How did they react?"

"I talked to her."

"Julia?"

"Yeah, I talked to Julia. She thanked me for the offer and asked if she could call me back. She wanted to talk to her husband first, see if they could work it out."

"He wasn't there? Where was the husband?"

Mrs. Garrity paused for another hit of oxygen. "I don't know," she said, when she'd taken several breaths. "I couldn't see. She was in her living room and I was in mine. We did not have Skype then."

"I just wondered if she mentioned where he was."

"It was the middle of the morning in the middle of the work week. He had a job. I'd imagine he was at work."

"Okay. But they called you back and accepted your offer?" he persisted.

"She called me back," the old lady said. "She was sweet and grateful and thanked me very nicely."

"And she said they'd come?"

"She said that she and Jude would come down. John had to stay in Portland until he finished working Friday. Julia and Jude came on Thursday morning. They stopped by my office and picked up the key. They said John would be here Friday night."

———♥———

"You'll eat something? Real food, I mean. I don't want you subsisting on bologna sandwiches."

John smiled down at her, amused. "I *can* feed myself. I was a bachelor during college, you know."

"I know. That's why I said no bologna."

He was leaning in the driver's window of her car. The trunk was loaded with clothing for all three of them and there was an ice chest beside Jude's car seat in the back. John wore a brown suit with a plain white shirt and a dark green tie. Pastel colors were fashionable, but his boss was an elderly man and old-fashioned in his sensibilities. John was freshly showered and shaven. His hair was damp, his cheeks pink from the razor, and he smelled like hair oil and aftershave. He kissed the tip of his index finger and tapped it against the end of her nose.

"I'll be fine. Have fun. I'll see you tomorrow, when I get off work."

"We'll miss you."

"I'll miss you more."

———♥———

"Hey there, Mrs. Garrity! It's supper time. Do you want to walk to the dining room or shall I get a wheelchair?"

Donaldson glared at the young nurse aide but she ignored him.

"I can walk," the old woman said. "Help me up, Dear."

The aide shouldered the bag the oxygen tank was in, then levered Mrs. Garrity up with a smooth, practiced motion. "Are your visitors going to sit with you while you eat?"

"No," she said. "They have business to take care of." She turned to Donaldson, snagging his sleeve when the younger woman would have led her out. "You *find* who killed that girl."

Donaldson's mouth tightened and the corner of his lips turned down. When he answered, there was a snide irony in his tone.

"Yes, ma'am."

He and Min left, heading back down the hall towards the exit and the parking lot beyond, but Julia lingered and watched the old woman and the young woman, intertwined, receding along the corridor.

Everyone had gotten old on her. Her mother and Mrs. Garrity and Alex Trebek. It made her think about John and about Jude. In her mind's eye, her husband was still as young as she was, their son a sweet-faced toddler. Intellectually she knew that was no longer the case and, as badly as she wanted to see them, she also did not.

———♥———

So far as she was able to remember, Julia had never been up the hill to the Millers' house.

Min was gone, returned to patrol for the rest of her shift, and Julia rode in the front seat of Donaldson's odd vehicle. It had a TV screen attached to a rear camera that came on when he put it in reverse, a remote control to unlock the doors, and a fancy radio with a CD slot instead of a cassette tape drawer. When he received a phone call--a local newspaper reporter fishing for information about Julia's murder--he answered it by pushing a button on the steering wheel. He spoke into thin air and the caller's voice came out of the stereo.

He followed the coast road back towards the vacation cabin. They passed the abandoned general store and the line of other cabins and Julia turned in her seat and splayed her fingers against the window glass as they cruised slowly past the one she and John always rented. She was having trouble working out the date, but it was summer. A family was just moving in. Two men and a woman carried duffel bags and ice chests in from a battered old Jeep while a trio of children danced and bounced around the front yard.

Donaldson guided his car across the parking area. The Millers' gate was still there, but it stood open. The gatepost it was attached to sagged and there were grass and weeds growing around the bottom of the gate itself so that Julia doubted it would even close anymore. There was a NO TRESPASSING sign on the right-hand post, but Donaldson ignored it and drove straight through.

The drive curved and climbed for better than a city block. There was a band of trees at the bottom, red alder and hemlock and big leaf maple. Then, as the path rose, it ran alongside a fenced-in pasture. There was a big feeder in a clearing near the top and it opened into a corral and a loading chute, but there were no animals in sight. A small, red barn at the crest of the hill had an abandoned, disused air about it and a henhouse a little further on was likewise deserted.

The house was a one-story farmhouse style building with a wide porch across the front. It could have used a new coat of paint. The lawn around it was overlong and dotted with dandelions gone to seed. A garden patch visible off to the side lay fallow.

Donaldson parked in the yard behind a battered pickup. Julia hurried after him when he got out, sliding out the driver's door just before he slammed it closed. She had not figured out how to pass through solid objects of her own volition even though, if he got too far away with the heart pendant, she would be dragged through anything that was between them.

He mounted the steps. Before he reached the last one the door opened and Harriet Miller stood there, blocking it like a linebacker and looking concerned.

She wasn't that different from the younger version of herself who lived in Julia's memory. A large, physically imposing woman, she had soft, anxious eyes in a stern face. Her hair, once brown, was now iron gray, but she still wore it in a bun on top of her head. She was dressed in faded jeans and a flowered tee shirt. There was flour on her left cheek and two white handprints on the sides of her shirt. She frowned at Donaldson, her lips pursed and her heavy eyebrows lowering and coming together.

"Can I help you?"

"Mrs. Miller?"

"Yes?"

"I'm Lieutenant Donaldson, with the Sheriff's Department. Is your husband home? I need to speak with the two of you."

"My husband's not well. This isn't a good day. Can you come back tomorrow?"

"I'm sorry," Donaldson said, not sounding it, "but no. I'm investigating a murder. I need to speak to the both of you now."

Harriet's mouth tightened but she held the door open and stood back. Donaldson nodded to her curtly as he stepped through. Julia darted after. They were in a shadowy living room, furnished with mismatched pieces. There was a window air conditioner, but it was turned off. The unencumbered windows were closed and the room stuffy. A large shelf held books and knick-knacks and the rear wall was covered with framed photographs. Everything was coated with a light sheen of dust.

They passed an open door on the left and Julia looked in on a spacious bedroom, dim behind closed curtains. Another window air conditioner sat silent. The bed was unmade and a bedside table contained a dirty glass, a scattering of used tissues and a collection of prescription pill bottles. There was a medicinal smell in the air and the whole place felt still and as if it were waiting for something.

A doorway in the back wall led into a kitchen. A table and four chairs took up the center of the room. There were dishes in the sink and the faded linoleum was worn in a path that led from the door to the refrigerator, and down in front of the sink and stove. A second door led out onto a screened-in back porch. The threshold had been replaced with a soft rubber bar. The outline of the original was still visible on either side of it. Charlie sat in a wheelchair on the porch with his back to them. He didn't look up as they came out.

"Please, can't you come back tomorrow?" Harriet pleaded. "This isn't a good day. It's a bad anniversary."

"Your marital issues aren't my problem," Donaldson said.

"It's not that kind of anniversary." Charlie's voice was thin and faint, threaded with whistling breaths. He spoke without turning, his gaze focused beyond the porch railing and the ocean and the edge of the world. "Fifty years ago today I was captured by the North Vietnamese."

"Oh, Charlie." Julia circled Harriet and Donaldson and went to lean on the rail just in front of him. He wore a loose white cotton tee shirt that made the deep burned red of his arms and chest that much more prominent. He was still bald, as she remembered, but at some point he'd grown a beard and mustache. It was snow white, patchy and bedraggled, missing chunks. Like Mrs. Garrity, he carried an oxygen tank tucked in beside him. There was a soft fleece throw over his legs and a little dog lay contentedly atop that. He stroked it absentmindedly with a shaking hand.

"We were on patrol in the jungle. Hotter'n hell, dripping with sweat. Humidity was so high, it was like walking through a cloud. Water dropping off the trees and running down your back. Swarms of tiny, stinging insects. I was nineteen. Hell, our squad leader was only twenty. We walked right into an ambush. The first I knew something was wrong was when a grenade blew up the guy three steps ahead of me. Palmer. His name was Palmer. Blast knocked me on my ass in the underbrush. I'm painted with gore. Palmer's blood and brains and whatnot. I look up and there's an enemy soldier standing over me, looking down his gunsight at me. I'll never forget that feeling of knowing you're about to die. It's like drowning. Right in that instant, I'd have done anything for just one more breath."

"Then what happened?" Donaldson asked, his voice hushed.

Charlie put up a trembling hand and traced a thin, white scar that marked his left cheek and his forehead above his eye. "He reversed his rifle and hit me with the butt. Smashed me in the face, like you'd kill a bug. I remember seeing it coming at me, then a blinding flash of light and then nothing. I woke up hanging by my arms in a room in the Hanoi Hilton."

"A hotel room?"

"Not a hotel," Harriet said, her own voice quiet. "The Hoa Lo Prison. It was a POW camp. Hanoi Hilton was a nickname."

"Oh, I see. Then what happened?"

Charlie came back from whatever distance he had been occupying and turned to look Donaldson in the eye.

"Things I don't talk about. Do I know you?"

"Ah, we've met. It's been awhile. I'm Lieutenant Donaldson, with the Lincoln County Sheriff's Department. I'm here about Julia Lodge."

"After all these years?"

"Haven't you seen the news lately?"

It was Harriet who answered. "We don't turn the TV on much. What happened?"

"Her body has been found."

Harriet dropped into a plastic lawn chair as if her knees had failed her. "Good heavens. Where?"

"In a cave on the coast. It's connected to the ocean by an underwater channel. We believe she was dumped in the ocean and an undercurrent carried her into the cave."

"Could she have drowned?"

"No. We're still waiting on the autopsy results, but there's definite evidence of foul play. You two were the last ones to see her alive. I need you to tell me about it."

"But we told you all this years ago," Charlie protested.

"I know. But now I need you to tell me again. What happened the night Julia Lodge disappeared?"

Chapter Eight

Didn't We Almost Have It All

[Whitney Houston, 1987]

Charlie dropped his head back against the back of his chair and closed his eyes. It looked as if he'd simply dropped off to sleep in the middle of their conversation. His lips were tinted dark blue and his skin, under the radiation burns was pale. It gave him the appearance of a figure molded in clay.

"Mr. Miller?" Donaldson prompted.

"I know," he said softly. "I know. I'm thinking. Give me a minute."

"Of course." Donaldson glanced at his watch. "Take your time."

"I saw her earlier that day, you know. Her and the boy. Down in the woods."

"That was Thursday, right? The day they arrived?"

"Thursday. Yeah. I guess it was. I was mushroom hunting down over the hill. She and the boy went looking for blackberries and got turned around. They come fighting their way out of the underbrush onto my path as I was making my way home. I was a bit cross with her, I think. I've always felt bad about that."

"Why were you cross with her?"

"There were some rattlesnakes, had a den in the rocks on the side of the hill. The way they came, she and the boy must have passed within five or six feet of them. It scared me, thinking they could have gotten bit."

"If you knew they were there, why didn't you shoot them?" Donaldson asked. "The snakes, I mean."

"We don't just wantonly kill things, Detective," Harriet replied, heat in her voice. "Snakes are part of nature. They have a right to live too. And they're harmless if you leave them alone. You're more likely to die of a dog bite than a snake bite in America. Did you know that? Providing you get treatment. Of course, you can still die if you can't get help, and that can be hard to come by when you're lost in the woods. Especially back then, when we didn't all have phones in our pockets."

"I also," Charlie cut in, regret in his voice, "I also had a bit of pot on me. Just a few leaves, in the top of one of my sacks of mushrooms. I was getting chemo for the first time then and pot helps with the side effects. I may have left that out the first time I told this, but I expect the statute of limitations has expired by now."

"I'm not interested in your Mary Jane," Donaldson said. "When you met Julia and her son in the woods, how did she seem to you? Was she sad? Upset? Frightened? Worried?"

"No. No, not at all. She seemed happy. Carefree. They'd been picking blackberries. Her little boy was covered in berry juice, his face and his hands and all over his shirt. She had half a bowlful left. He kept trying to get to them and she was trying to hang on to enough to bake with. I walked them down to the gate to their cottage. She said she was going to make muffins. She promised to bring me some."

"Was anyone else there, that you saw? Did you notice anyone hanging around?"

He tipped his head and his gaze wandered off to the right. "There was a car in the parking area," he said, "and a young fella down on the beach with a metal detector. He made me uneasy. I don't know why. There wasn't anything unusual about it. But I warned Julia to be careful and I waited for them to get inside before I left. Probably didn't mean anything though."

"And that was the last time you saw them until they turned up at your house that night?"

"It was."

Charlie had a glass sitting on the porch rail beside his chair, some kind of pale amber liquid over ice. Tea, maybe, or apple juice. The ice was half melted. Condensation dripped off the outside of the glass and the contents were stratified into a layer of beverage and a layer of water. He paused to pick it up and drain it and Harriet rose immediately to take it into the kitchen and refill it.

"Detective? Can I offer you something to drink?"

"No, thank you." Donaldson fiddled with the notebook he held open on his knee. "Tell me about that night. What happened that night?"

"We were both asleep," Harriet said.

"We were stoned," Charlie corrected her. "Stoned and passed out. I'd been up and down, sick and vomiting half the night. Pounding on the door woke me up and I went to see what was going on. Harry came stumbling along a couple of minutes later."

"And it was Julia Lodge with her little boy?"

"Yeah. Yeah, it was."

"Was the boy awake when you answered the door?"

"No, asleep. Sound asleep on his momma's shoulder. She was upset. Looked like she'd been crying. Kept glancing over her shoulder at the car. She said there'd been a family emergency and asked me if we could watch her son for a few hours."

"That didn't seem strange to you? That she'd leave her son with relative strangers?"

"At the time, no. It was the middle of the night and I don't think either of us was thinking clear. In retrospect, yeah. Although, I suppose if she had to leave him with someone local, she knew us as well as anybody."

"What was she wearing?"

"Hell, I don't know."

"No? Nothing? An impression? A color? She did *have* clothes on?"

"Well, yeah. I'm pretty sure I'd have noticed if she didn't. But as for what, hell. I don't pay attention to women's clothes in broad daylight when I'm sober."

"It's true," Harriet agreed. "I could wear a trash bag and he wouldn't look twice."

50

Charlie patted her hand. "I would if I was looking for a trash bag."

"Tell me about the car," Donaldson said. "Was it Julia's car? Can you be sure?"

"It was a car," Charlie said, "but that's all I could tell you. I mean, it wasn't a truck or a van or a station wagon. But beyond that, your guess is as good as mine. The headlights were on, pointing at the house. The glare was blinding. It was a car and there was someone waiting by it. A man, I think."

"I thought it could have been her husband," Harriet said softly, looking down at her hands in her lap.

"It wasn't her husband," Charlie disagreed.

"How can you be sure?" Donaldson pressed. "If you couldn't see him clearly?"

"I knew her husband. Nice kid. He liked baseball. He'd come up a few times the summer before, sat and listened to Mariners games with me. I'd have known him if I'd seen him. It wasn't him."

"But you said yourself it was dark and late. You were stoned. The headlights were in your eyes."

"It could have been him," Harriet said persuasively. "Can't we just agree that it could have been him?"

"No. Because it wasn't." Charlie's tone left no room for doubt.

Harriet shrugged, a tiny movement that barely shifted her shoulders. Her eyes stayed down. "You're probably right," she said with no conviction.

"Is there anything else we can help you with, Detective?" Charlie asked.

"Ah, yeah, actually. We believe her body was dumped in the ocean. Do you know of anywhere around here where someone could find a boat on short notice?"

Charlie laughed without amusement. "Yeah. Down on the beach at the foot of our stairs."

"I don't follow you?"

"We had a boat. A little wooden rowboat, just to mess around in. Kept it turned over on the sand below the bluff. Kept it there for years. It eventually got dry rot and we let some teenagers use it for a bonfire, but in '86 it should've still been seaworthy. All anybody had to do was flip it over and drag it into the surf."

"Wouldn't you have noticed if someone had taken it out?"

"Not if they put it back. Hell, I didn't look at the thing for months at a time."

Charlie paused to take a drag from the oxygen tank. His voice had gotten thready and his thin shoulders shook under the t-shirt material.

"My husband needs his rest, Mister Donaldson," Harriet said. "Are you going to be much longer?"

He flipped his notebook closed and stood. "No, I think that should be everything for now. I'll be in touch if I have any more questions."

"Of course." Harriet rose as well. "I'll see you out."

She led the way back through the twilight house. It wasn't until Donaldson was half outside, holding the screen door, that she spoke again.

"Detective?"

He turned back. "Yes?"

"I really think that--"

The back door banged. Harriet froze in mid-sentence and she and Donaldson (and Julia) turned to look. Charlie had rolled himself into the kitchen and he sat there now, looking at his wife with no expression on his face.

She swallowed and fluttered her hands, turned back to Donaldson.

"I hope that you find what you're looking for," she said, and closed the door behind him.

———♥———

The camera in the forensic lab was designed to record autopsies. It provided a perfect view of Julia's bones laid out on the table, but only the tops of the heads of the men standing next to it.

"I also recorded the conversation," Min said, laying a small silver device next to the computer monitor she, Donaldson, Oliver, and, unbeknownst to the cops, Julia was watching.

"Did you tell them you were recording?" Donaldson asked.

"Yes, it's on the record. Was I not supposed to?"

"It might have been more revealing if you hadn't," he said, "but at least this way we can use it in court if we need to."

Jude, full-grown, towered over his father, a fact that was only apparent because when they embraced his dark head hid John's gray one. Min's voice came from the recording device.

"I'm going to record this conversation for the record," she said. "First of all, I'm very sorry for your loss."

"Thank you." Her son's familiar voice, deepened into maturity, sent chills down Julia's spine.

"Are you sure it's her?" John asked.

"The medical examiner is going to compare her dental records to be sure," Min said, "but we found this with her body." She held out her phone.

"Her necklace."

"You recognize it?"

"Yes. We gave it to her, Jude and I. Where did you find her? Do you know...do you know how she died?"

"We haven't determined a cause of death yet," the young deputy said carefully. "Her body was in a cave above the beach, less than a mile from the beach house where you were staying. There's a tidal pool connected to the sea through an underwater channel. We think her body washed in from the ocean."

In the video, John reached out a trembling hand and cradled Julia's skull. When he spoke it was a single word. Less than a whisper, more than a breath. "Sweetheart."

With tears on her own cheeks, Julia reached out towards the image. The picture buzzed and jumped and the recorder skipped and she drew back quickly.

"What did you do," Min asked, "when you realized she was missing?"

"I looked for her."

"Looked where?"

"The old man--Charlie Miller? Charlie Miller told me she came by his house in the middle of the night with some man driving her car and told him there was a family emergency. The first thing I thought was that something happened to her mother and her family sent someone down to get her. There wasn't a phone at the beach house, so they'd have had to drive down. But when I went to a phone booth and started calling them, no one knew anything."

"You went to a phone booth," Min said. "You didn't have your phone with you?"

In the sheriff's department Donaldson snorted and Min's cheeks pinked. "I wasn't thinking," she defended herself.

On the tape, John answered her kindly. "We didn't have cell phones then. Mobile phones existed but they were huge and expensive. Something rich people carried."

"Right. I'm sorry. I knew that."

"Dad reported her missing right away," Jude said. "Or he tried to. They wouldn't take a report until she'd been missing two days and then that asshole cop didn't do anything anyway for months."

"Donaldson?" Min asked.

"Yeah. Him."

Donaldson gave her an annoyed look. "Asshole cop?" he asked.

"I knew you were the one who took the report," she said defensively, her blush deepening.

Oliver made a face and looked away, biting back a laugh.

"When you couldn't find her, what then?"

John's shoulders moved and when he spoke he sounded as helpless as Julia had ever heard him. "I kept looking. I went to every gas station in a fifty mile radius to ask if anyone remembered her. I went to all the other vacation houses to see if anyone saw a strange car that night. We put up flyers and organized searches. I walked the headlands and called her name. She was just gone. Gone like she was never there."

He turned beneath the camera and as he reached up to lay a hand alongside his son's face she caught, just for a second, his familiar profile.

"It wasn't supposed to be like this," he said. "This isn't

what the future was supposed to hold for us. We were going to have more kids. Laugh and dance. Sit up all night talking and make love in the rain. We were going to grow old together and spoil our grandchildren."

He was shaking. Even in the poor-quality video she could see that. Jude reached out for him, encircled him in his arms and gathered him in as if he were the adult and John the child. When he spoke again his voice was muffled against their son's chest.

"I want my wife back."

Chapter Nine

When Doves Cry

[Prince and the Revolution, 1984]

"What are you?"

Donaldson leaned his butt against the side of Min's desk and looked down at her critically. It was a dreary, sopping wet afternoon and Donaldson and his helpers were spending it reviewing thirty-year-old witness interviews recorded on dusty cassette tapes. The tapes were almost the first familiar things Julia had seen since waking up in the cave. Rather than alleviating her sense of alienation, seeing them juxtaposed against cellphones and laptop computers accentuated it.

Halloween had been and gone. Julia's calendar was the progression of construction paper decorations Chris Oliver's kids made for his desk and Min's and some of the other deputies' but never for Donaldson's. Right now it was cheerful turkeys with their names written in crayon in a childish hand.

Oliver had ventured out into the stormy noonday, to pick up the takeout they'd ordered for lunch, leaving Min alone with their superior.

"What?" she asked, confused.

"What are you?" he repeated. Her blank look didn't change and he gave a short, sharp shake of his head. "Where are you from?"

"Klamath Falls."

"No, I mean originally."

"Klamath Falls. I was born there."

"Okay, but you're some flavor of Asian, right? What are you? Chinese? Vietnamese? Szechuan?"

She sighed and rolled her eyes. "My parents are from South Korea," she said.

"Oh, yeah? What brought them to the U.S.?"

"They came here in 1990 to pick mushrooms."

"You're kidding."

"No, really."

"Mushrooms."

"Yeah. Mushrooms."

"They don't have mushrooms in Korea?"

"Not as many as they have here. When the nuclear reactor at Chernobyl blew up, one of the things it did was wipe out the eastern Asian mushroom crops. The prices skyrocketed and it became a way to make good money. My parents were just out of school and newlyweds. They came as a kind of an adventure. They started down in California and worked their way up the coast, following the season. They lived in tent cities with other pickers. It was all before I was born, but the way they tell it it sounds pretty hippie."

"Oh, I remember the crazy mushroom people. We had to check that they had valid licenses and enforce the daily limits if they didn't. I didn't pay that much attention, though. I figured they were mostly beaners. Never guessed some of them were coming all the way from Asia. So I guess that makes you their little fungus, doesn't it?"

The door opening cut off any reply she might have been going to make and Oliver came back in dripping and carrying two big paper sacks and a drink holder with three cups in it. The bags smelled like sausage and tomato sauce, like garlic and onion and fresh-baked bread.

Julia wanted a sandwich. She wanted a cup of coffee or a soda, a banana split, a goddamn glass of water. She missed her house and her car and her family and her *life*.

"It's a fuckin' lake out there," Oliver said. His left leg was soaked from mid-calf down and he was limping. He dropped the bags and drink carrier on Min's desk and sank into his own chair, pulling open his bottom drawer and retrieving a balled up pair of black socks. "At this rate, I'm going to run out of dry clothes."

He fought, for a minute, with the wet laces, then toed the shoe off and stripped off his wet sock. Donaldson, a sub sandwich halfway to his mouth, froze and made a strangled noise in the back of his throat.

"Something you want to share with the class there, buddy-boy?"

Oliver's toenails were petal pink.

He glanced down and laughed. "Oh, yeah. Maisie wanted us to paint our toenails this morning. I didn't have time to clean them off before work."

"You let her paint your toenails?"

"Hey, if a three-year-old thinks daddy needs pretty toenails, daddy's gonna have pretty damn toenails. You try explaining to a toddler that you're too macho to be pretty."

"You could just beat her ass and make her do what you say," Donaldson suggested.

Oliver froze, a dry sock scrunched up in his hand, ready for him to slide his foot into it. He turned and gave Donaldson a level look. "Is that what you did?"

Donaldson straightened and pulled himself up to his full height. "What do you mean by that?"

"I'm just asking. You're giving me child rearing advice. I'd just like to know where it's coming from."

For maybe twenty seconds Donaldson didn't move, then he spun abruptly, grabbing his drink off Min's desk and speaking over his shoulder. "I don't have time for this shit. I've got things to do. I'll be in my office. Don't bother me unless it's an emergency."

The door slammed behind him and Oliver slipped his sock on in silence. He found a roll of paper towels and stuffed his wet shoe with them, then hopped over to Min's desk to retrieve his own lunch.

Min, wide-eyed with wonder, glanced around to make sure no one was within earshot. They were alone but even so she leaned over her desk and whispered. "What was that all about?"

Oliver, clearly still agitated, set his soda cup down with more force than was strictly necessary. "You know he's got a kid, right?"

"Oh, God. No. He spawned?"

Her horrified tone drew a chuckle from him. "A son," he clarified. "He's in his early twenties. He's a minor-league hockey player, actually. Hot stuff. Top prospect. Future superstar."

"So how come we don't hear about him twenty-four/seven?"

"Because Donaldson hasn't seen him in years. Kid uses his mother's last name. Won't give Donaldson the time of day." Oliver settled back into his chair and his shoulders slumped. "That was probably below the belt," he admitted, "but I don't care. He doesn't get an opinion about how I raise my kids and nobody--and I mean *nobody*--gets to ever joke about hitting my daughter."

—♥—

"Can you give me an official cause of death?"

They were back at the state crime lab, in Clackamas. Julia's bones had been cleaned and laid out on one of the tables in a semblance of the order they'd occupied in her body. They weren't all there and many of the ones that were there were broken. Someone had glued her teeth back into her skull.

Min stood somberly beside the table, her posture stiff and uncomfortable looking. Her face was puffy and her clothes tight and Julia had seen her, back at the sheriff's department, slipping tampons out of a desk drawer and into her pocket.

Dalton, the M.E., stood across from her. Donaldson was pacing restlessly, agitated. He stopped every few minutes to fiddle with this or that piece of equipment and Dalton tensed every time he did.

"Blunt force trauma," Dalton said. "A single blow to the back of the head. It would have destroyed the medulla oblongata, the bulge at the top of the spinal cord that controls vital functions. She'd have died almost immediately." He reached out with a gloved hand to turn her skull so they could see the hole at the base.

He handled her remains gently, with respect, and Julia wished she could tell him she appreciated it.

Donaldson was across the lab with his back to them,

running one finger idly over an expensive-looking microscope. He turned at the waist to scowl back at Dalton. "I thought you said it was a gunshot wound?"

"I thought it was, at first glance. That's why we do autopsies. There's a pattern of microfractures around the wound that's consistent with a blow rather than a bullet. And, of course, there's no exit wound and you've found no slug."

"It could have washed away," Donaldson said, though Julia had heard him deny that very same possibility to the sheriff.

"Maybe. Unlikely though, and I think you know that. Her teeth didn't and a slug would have been heavier and protected inside the skull. Is there a reason you had your heart set on a bullet wound?"

"He has no heart," Julia said. From the expression on Min's face, she guessed the young deputy was thinking the same thing.

"No," Donaldson said, turning to face them finally and walking over. "It's just, I've been trying to figure out where Lodge could have gotten a gun."

"My husband didn't kill me," Julia ground out. "How could you even think that?"

"One of his co-workers reported a burglary a couple of months before she went missing. One of the things stolen was a handgun."

"Oh." Dalton shook his head. "Well, sorry to disappoint you, but she wasn't shot."

Donaldson's frown turned thoughtful. "Blunt force trauma...like a baseball bat?"

Julia bristled. John had carried a bat in the trunk of his car since she'd known him. He played baseball.

"I suppose it's possible," Dalton conceded. "If the bat had a nail or something driven into it and sticking out an inch or so. I don't think it's likely, though. A bat with a nail in it would have likely left behind a band of cracked bone. A point of contact for the barrel of the bat as well as a hole from the nail."

"What then?"

"A chisel, maybe? A small, hand-held pickax? A high-heeled shoe even. Bring me a weapon and I'll tell you if it fits."

"Hmph." Donaldson stood over the table, looking down at Julia's bones. "She sure looks different than the last time I saw her."

"In the cave?" Min asked.

"No, before that. I mean when she was alive."

Her eyebrows rose and her voice took on a note of sympathy. "You knew the victim?"

Dalton snorted and turned away.

"Go on," Julia taunted from behind Donaldson. "Go on and tell her. Tell her how you knew me."

"You could say that," Donaldson admitted at last.

"What was she like?"

He shrugged. "She was hot." He looked the young deputy up and down, allowing the hint of a sneer. "Hotter than you. I'd have done her."

"Never in a million years," Julia said. She stepped close to him, glowering, and he shivered a little and shifted away.

"So how did you know her then?"

"Yeah, Donaldson. How did you know her?" In spite of his question, it was clear Dalton knew the story.

"That's not important," Donaldson said, brushing off the question. "It has nothing to do with our investigation."

"Oh, go on and tell her," the coroner scoffed. "She's going to hear it eventually anyway. This way you can get your side in first."

Min was waiting expectantly. Donaldson huffed out a breath and ran a hand through his hair.

"Fine. If you must know, I arrested her. For prostitution."

Min's eyes widened. "She was a hooker?"

Donaldson's mouth tightened like he'd bitten into something sour, the same expression he'd made when he'd had to unlock the cell and let Julia leave, and he scowled at her. "No."

"But then...?"

"It was my first month on the job, okay? The first shift I worked without a training officer, in fact. And I see this couple together on the beach. Young Black bitch, hotter than hell, with her hair all done and makeup on, wearing a skimpy little outfit that barely covered her ass--"

"It was a shorts set," Julia seethed. "It was just a shorts set. I got it at JC Penney. There were twenty white women on that beach wearing less than I was and you came straight after me."

"--and she's with this scruffy young guy in beat-up blue jeans and an old baseball jersey. Naturally, I thought it was a hooker and her john. So I arrest her--let him go with a warning. You'd think he'd appreciate that. Half an hour later he shows up at the station with a marriage license, so I had to let her go."

"You didn't tell her the best part," Dalton said. Donaldson glared at him but he ignored him and continued. "Julia Lodge's father was a retired journalism professor. One of his former students heard what happened and used it as the centerpiece for a series of articles on systemic racism in police departments. The detective here became the poster boy for racist cops in Oregon. The fact that he was so new helped him out, if I remember. But it was quite the scandal for a while there. What all did you have to do to keep your badge? Apologize, attend sensitivity training."

"That obviously didn't take," Julia interceded.

"Weren't you on probation for a few months there?"

"Which was complete bullshit," Donaldson seethed. "They made a big deal of it because of the negative publicity, but there wasn't a cop on the force who wouldn't have come to the same conclusion that I did."

Min hesitated and bit her lip but spoke up. "Isn't that racial profiling?"

"It's police work. Look! Do you know why we arrest hookers? We're not the fun police. It's not because we're uptight about morals or we don't want anyone to have a good time. Prostitution is *dangerous*. Hookers get killed every day. I arrested her because my instincts--I have *very* good instincts--were telling me that John Lodge was a threat to her. I arrested her because I could tell she was in danger."

"And you think you were right?"

He snatched up one of Julia's leg bones and waved it in Min's face. "You think I was wrong?"

"But it was years later that she disappeared."

"She got lucky. Her luck ran out. Julia's family was upper middle class, well-educated, she moved in higher social circles than he did. At least before her marriage. He was blue-collar, devout Catholic, the first one in his family to even go to college. She was smart, beautiful, popular, obviously married beneath herself. Did you know she had a degree in chemical engineering? Before she got pregnant she was planning to go to grad school. She could have gotten a job making ten times what he pulled in, but instead she quit school to stay home and play housewife."

"My choices are none of your business," Julia snarled at him.

"And John was manipulative. He kept her apart. Isolated her."

"He did not! That never happened!"

"He worked for a family-owned company that manufactured safety equipment. It was a small business, close-knit. They had company dinners at least once a month, picnics, baseball games. The Lodges never once attended, in spite of the owner inviting John every time. He was the only employee who never brought his family to one of those functions. All his co-workers testified to that."

"I don't know what you're talking about," Julia said. "John never mentioned any picnics or dinners. But if there were such a thing and he didn't want to go, I'm sure he had a good reason."

She was troubled, though. She didn't think they had secrets from one another. Why wouldn't he have at least mentioned these gatherings, even if he didn't want to attend? And why wouldn't he have wanted to go? The only explanation she could think of was that he was having problems with a co-worker. But, again, why wouldn't he have said something? The only one of his co-workers she'd even met was the company owner, and that just one time. He was a sweet-faced little old man with a shock of white hair and a grandfatherly demeanor. He reminded her of a Care Bear and it seemed to her that it would have been nice to spend some time with him and the work family he'd gathered around him. Still...

"John wouldn't hurt me," she insisted.

"They lost touch with their college friends," Donaldson continued.

"Most of them moved away. They had jobs and families. We still wrote and talked on the phone from time to time."

"The only person they really socialized with was John Lodge's younger sister, Belle."

"There's nothing wrong with that!"

"The last time Julia was seen was when she left her son at the Miller's during the late night or early morning of August 7-8, 1986. Thursday night or Friday morning. John had stayed behind in Portland, ostensibly to finish out the work week, and was supposed to join them Friday night. That's what Julia told the old lady. You heard for yourself when she told me."

Min nodded to show she was following along.

"But John Lodge finished his week's work early Thursday afternoon. He bought a bottle of wine and a dozen roses and went home and changed clothes. At 5:27 he received a phone call from a pay phone in the Corvallis area. At a little after 9 A.M. Friday morning he turned up at the vacation cottage claiming to be looking for his family."

"This makes no sense," Julia said.

"Well, where did he go?" Min asked.

"I don't know. I can damn well guess, but I don't know."

"What does he say?"

"Nothing! Okay? John Lodge says nothing. For three decades now, he's stood on his fifth amendment right to remain silent and he has not said a single word about where he went or what he did."

"This doesn't make sense," Julia repeated. "It's crazy. This is all crazy."

"Why haven't you arrested him?" Min wanted to know.

"How can I? All I have is circumstantial evidence. I can't put him within a hundred miles of this place that night. If I could get Harriet Miller to testify that John was the one with

Julia that night, and if Charlie wasn't around to contradict her, maybe I could get the DA to file charges. The old man's pretty sick. I'm hoping he'll die soon. But for now, it's just not feasible. Because there *are* other explanations for where he might have gone and what he might have been doing."

"Like what?"

"The most obvious is that he was having an affair. He did buy wine and roses, remember"

"But wouldn't he come clean when he was suspected of murder?"

"Not if he was protecting the other woman. Or, hell, other man for that matter. But if it were a case of him actually being convicted? If we try him without knowing where he was and what he was doing and he produces an iron-clad alibi, all we'll have done is wasted taxpayer money and looked like fools in a high-profile case. And remember that District Attorneys are elected. No one wants to give their opponent that kind of ammunition."

"What does Belle say?" Julia asked. "Whatever John was doing, Belle will know. She'll tell you if she knows you think he killed me."

"What does his sister say?" Min echoed Julia as if she could hear her. "You said they were close? Has anyone asked her what she knows?"

"Funny you should ask that," Donaldson said. "I *did* talk to her, way back in '86, when I was just starting this investigation. It was the day before her wedding."

"Belle got married?" Julia asked. The last she knew, Belle wasn't even dating anyone.

"I spoke to her in the afternoon, while her mother finished hemming her wedding gown. They were in a hurry to get done so they wouldn't be late to the rehearsal dinner."

"And what did she say?"

"Not much. I was right at the beginning of the investigation and I didn't know yet about John's disappearing act. I could tell she was fighting nerves, but I thought it was just the wedding."

"Didn't you go back and talk to her later?"

"No. I couldn't. Because that night she overdosed on sleeping pills. I asked her about her missing sister-in-law and that same night, the night before her wedding, Belle Lodge killed herself."

Chapter Ten

Lost In Love

[Air Supply, 1979]

The carpet in the squad room at the Lincoln County Sheriff's Office was dark grey with a low pile that barely cushioned the concrete floor beneath. Julia sat in the corner, wedged between a wall and a filing cabinet, with her nightshirt pulled down over her knees to her bare toes and her face buried in her folded arms.

Lowering storm clouds sent sheets of driving rain against the window. She wept and the sky wept with her.

———♥———

The first time she'd seen Belle Lodge she'd been a 21-year-old college senior and Belle had been a 17-year-old high school junior. Julia was a campus ambassador. Being the sole occupant of a double room made it easy for her to host prospective students for a three-day visit.

Julia and an aide from the admissions office had met Belle and her parents in the dorm lobby when they arrived. Her first impression of the younger girl was that she was shy and painfully withdrawn. She wore a Catholic school girl's uniform, with her blond hair pulled back into a severe ponytail.

Her parents were both short, sturdy individuals, conservatively dressed, with matching dour expressions. Her mother had on a flowered dress that Julia was guessing was home-made and her father wore work pants and a blue-collar shirt with a wrench logo on both sleeves and his name in a patch on the left breast. When they met Julia she could see the shock and dismay on both their faces.

"Are you sure you don't want to just come back home?" the mother asked Belle. "You know we won't be able to afford sending you here. This is nothing but a waste of time."

"There are lots of options for financing," the admissions aide said cheerfully, either oblivious to the tensions or pretending to be. She was a bouncy preppie, not more than a couple of years out of school herself. She wore a green sweater over a pink polo shirt and khakis, with big earrings and poufy dark hair. The sweater was loosely knit and the alligator on her shirt breast peeked through between the strands of yarn. "Why don't we let her decide if she even wants to attend first?"

Belle spoke softly and her tone was respectful, but she lifted her chin and dug in her heels. "I do want to do this. Besides, it would be rude of me to waste the opportunity after Dad took off work this morning to drive me down here."

"He'll just have to take off again in three days to come get you. Did you think of that?"

"Do what you're going to do," the father said. "I have to get back so I can go to work this afternoon."

Belle took a deep breath and shouldered the worn duffel bag she was carrying. "I'll see you in three days," she said, and resolutely turned her back on them.

"I'll take good care of her," Julia assured her parents, and led her away.

"I'm sorry about my folks,' Belle said, when they were safely inside Julia's room.

"Didn't expect to have to leave you with a Black girl, did they?" Julia asked, amused. She was too used to this type of reaction to even be bitter about it anymore. Much.

Belle's fair face reddened but she had the grace not to deny it. "No, I guess not. But they don't want me to go to college anyway. They want me to marry a nice Catholic boy and have his children and settle down to be a good little housewife."

"What do you want?"

Belle looked her directly in the eye then and broke out into a smile so beautiful it was breathtaking. "I want to talk to dolphins," she said.

"Really?"

"Really! Or whales. Or *and* whales. I want to be an oceanographer. Did you know 71% of the Earth's surface is covered by water? And we've barely explored any of it. We have *so much* to learn!"

"That's fantastic," Julia said. "You can do that. Don't let anyone tell you that you can't."

Belle set her bag down on the bed Julia had pointed her to. "Do you mind if I change?"

"Not at all."

Belle pulled the fastener out of her hair and let it settle around her shoulder and took a set of clothes out of the bag. "My folks don't even know I own these clothes," she confided. "John bought them for me and snuck them into the house while Dad was at work and Mom was at a church committee meeting."

While she was talking, she unbuttoned her blouse and pulled it off. A crystal prism dangled from a blue ribbon around her neck, nestled between her breasts. Hidden beneath the uniform. It caught the light coming in the window and scattered rainbows across the room. In later years, Julia remembered that specific moment as the instant when her entire life changed.

"John?" she asked.

"My big brother. He goes here too. He's a senior. I don't suppose you know him?"

"It's a big campus. What's his major?"

"Business, but he also plays baseball. He's here on a baseball scholarship."

"Oh. I'm not much into sports. Is he any good?"

"I think he is. I think he's better than he thinks he is. He was scouted by the Phillies when he was in high school, you know? Our parents didn't encourage it, though. They're always on him to be responsible and get a reliable career. Something he can make money at. Dad says, 'dreams don't pay the light bill, son.'"

Belle changed into jeans and a scoop-necked blouse. She fluffed out her hair and pulled the crystal pendant out to let it lie on top of her clothes. Trusting her heart to the world,

Julia thought.

"Your brother sounds like a nice guy," she said.

"I think you'd like him," Belle agreed. "Maybe I can introduce you while I'm here."

—♥—

"Oh, it ain't that bad, little missy."

Julia raked a hand down her face to wipe away tears and looked up. A strange man stood in the middle of the police station, looking down at her.

He was a tall guy, skinny and muscled, with brown hair and light eyes. His arms and face were burnt a deep, reddish-brown but paler skin showed beneath the sleeve of his tee shirt when he moved his arm. Everything about him was dirty and worn, from his greasy hair to his grungy boots. He loomed over her, but when she pulled herself to her feet he was no taller than she was. He spoke in a Cajun accent, his words full of gumbo and gators, Mardi Gras and zaideco music and dire secrets buried in Mississippi mud.

"Someone I care about is dead," Julia said.

"Lot of that going around. They go into the light?

"What light?"

The stranger rocked back on his heels and looked at her in surprise. "You din't get no light? I ain't never heered of no one who din't get a light."

"I don't know what you're talking about.

"Huh." He walked around in a circle in the middle of the room. Deputy Min was sitting at her desk, a steaming cup of coffee on the corner. The stranger passed her in the course of his pacing and, almost absentmindedly, reached out and lay a hand atop the cup. When he removed it the steam was gone. "Y'all know you're dead, right?"

Julia leaned against the filing cabinet, crossed her arms over her breast and wished, not for the first time, that she were wearing real clothes. "Yes, thank you. That did catch my attention."

"Whoa. Don't gotta be snippy there, little lady. I'm just trying to figure out what's going on."

"Who are you?"

"You kin call me Rex."

"Is that your name?"

"Does it matter?"

She cocked her head to the side, studying him. "No, I suppose not."

"And who might you have been when you were alive?"

"My name is Julia. Julia Lodge."

"Pleased to meetcha, Julia Lodge."

Ricky McFarlane, the department's K-9 officer, came in with his German shepherd-Rottweiler mix, Lando. Lando was big, calm and steady. Like most animals, he was aware of Julia, but unlike most he did not shy away from her. He didn't like Rex, though. He growled low in his throat. His hackles rose and he made a wide circle around the stranger.

McFarlane, leafing through a folder of papers, patted him absently.

"What light?" Julia asked again.

"Most folks, s'far's I know, a bright light shows up and follers 'em around when they die. Disappears behind 'em if'n they go into it. Hangs around fer about a week if'n they don't. You din't see one? How'd you bite it?"

Julia blinked. "I'm sorry?"

"Die, darlin'. Die. How'd you bite the big one?"

"I don't know."

"How can you not know?"

"I *don't know*," Julia said, frustrated. "I just...woke up dead."

"Huh." He made a show of thinking about it, then nodded towards Donaldson's door. "That yer boyfriend?"

"No. God, no! Why would you even think that?"

"Because yer tied to somethin' in that room."

"You can tell that?"

Rex shrugged. "You got a cord running from you through that door. You kin't see it?"

"No. I don't see anything."

"You sure don't know much about bein' dead."

"I'm sorry. I've never been dead before."

"There you go gettin' snippy again. You don't got to be

nasty. I's jest tryin' to help. I don't got to help if yer gone be nasty."

Julia forced herself to calm down and took at least the illusion of a deep breath. "I'm sorry. I'm under a lot of pressure right now and I'm just trying to figure out what's going on. What about you? Didn't you get a light? Why didn't you go into it?"

"Mind yer own business," he hissed.

"Look, I'm just wondering why you're here because I'm trying to figure out why I am."

"Jest don' be so nosy," Rex said. A rain jacket hung on a rack near the door--Donaldson's jacket, in fact. Rex went up to it and stared at it for a few seconds.

Julia found herself watching in wide-eyed amazement as he reached through the fabric into the jacket's pocket and drew out a set of keys.

"How did you do that?"

Rex smirked, pleased with himself. "I got skills, darlin'." He put his hand through the top of a filing cabinet and when he removed it the keys were gone.

"Okay, look. You reaching into the jacket is one thing. How did you get the keys out? You passed a physical object through another physical object."

"It's an illusion. It's all an illusion."

"You mean you didn't really reach in and take those keys?"

"No, I did that. I mean it's *all* an illusion. Everything. Stuff."

"Matter?"

"Yeah. Matter. Y'got to learn to look into things. It's like...water. Right? You just look at it and all you see is the surface. But if you look *into* it, you kin see what's under the surface. And then you kin change it to do what you want."

"But I can't even pick up things that aren't inside other things." Julia demonstrated, trying to close her fingers around a pencil on Oliver's desk and watching it slip through her incorporeal hand.

"Y'don't got the energy. Y'got to learn to harvest energy."

"How?"

Behind Julia, Min made a sudden noise of revulsion. Julia turned to find her setting her cup down with a moue of disgust. "Oh, my God. My coffee's totally cold."

Rex smirked.

"Wait! I get it now," Julia said. "When you put your hand over her coffee, you drained the thermal energy. It's like when I get close to something that has batteries and the batteries die."

"Right. People give off energy too, but it's usually not enough to do anything with unless they're really charged up. Happy, sad, pissed off. Or unless there's a lot of people. Find someplace with a lot of excited people sometime and you'll see what I mean. Lot more of our kind there too."

"Ghosts hang out in crowds?"

"Sure. Malls, amusement parks, ballfields, political rallies. Anywhere there's energy."

"And any kind of energy will do?"

"Some energy's better'n others. I wouldn't go up and put yer finger in a light socket. Strange things apt to happen if you put yer finger in a light socket."

"So I would imagine. So why are you here, in the police station, instead of at a mall or an amusement park?"

Rex grinned unpleasantly. One of the little folding computers that had become so ubiquitous sat unattended on a nearby desk. He lay his palm flat on the keyboard and Julia heard a faint electrical snap as the battery drained.

"I jest like to fuck wit' cops," he said.

———♥———

"Hey, Buddy! Mom tells me you have something exciting to tell me." The construction paper Christmas trees had given way to red-and-white hearts and when it rained now (because this was Oregon and it *always* rained) there was snow and sleet in the mix and ice like spun sugar coated the dark needles of the evergreen trees.

Julia sat at an empty desk, the deputy who belonged to it having clocked out and gone home hours before. Rex had moved on. She couldn't pretend to feel disappointed, but his tricks with the keys (Donaldson had hunted for them for days before he found them) intrigued her. She stared down at the wood, trying to do as he had said and look into it rather than just at its surface.

Oliver was on the phone to his kids, a nightly ritual he never missed when he was working, even if he sometimes had to call them a little early or a little late. "You *did*? That's so *awesome*!" He moved the phone aside to speak to his fellow cops. "Zack got all pluses on his report card!"

"He's in kindergarten," Donaldson said drily. "Did you think he was going to fail coloring?"

Julia had started trying to see into solid objects right after Rex took off. In moments of optimism, she thought she was making progress. In moments of despair she was sure she was imagining it.

Min leaned over to shout into the phone. "Zack! Can you hear me? It's Auntie Sarah! Your daddy said you got all pluses! I'm so proud of you!"

Oliver beamed and Donaldson rolled his eyes.

"Tell you what," Oliver reclaimed the conversation. "How about in the morning I make us some special turtle pancakes to celebrate? Heck yeah, with chocolate chips! You bet. Okay, you better get to bed now. I can hear you yawning from here. Sleep tight, Buddy. Remember I love you. Yes, I love you too. Okay, now. Put your sister on."

There were these optical illusion posters that had been popular when Julia was alive. She remembered seeing them the last time she went to the mall. At first glance, they were simply blankets of odd shapes, locked together in horizontal bands of color. But if you learned to look at them right they opened up into three dimensional images. You had to look into them, like looking into a window box. Belle had had one that was three dolphins swimming through an undersea landscape. Julia had stared at that thing for weeks without seeing it and then, one day, it was just suddenly there. The more you looked at them, the easier it got to see the picture. She'd even toyed with the idea of getting one for her own living room.

Death had intervened before she'd made up her mind.

"Maisie? Hi, sweetheart! It's Daddy!"

"Tell her you want your balls back," Donaldson suggested.

Oliver ignored him. "I just wanted to tell my favorite little girl good night…"

The top of the desks looked like oak, solid slabs set on gray metal frames. But when you looked closely you could see that they were some kind of pressed particle board with a thin sheet of oak veneer on top. Julia concentrated, looking into it like it was Belle's dolphin picture, and she could *almost see.* An intricate dance pulled atoms into molecules. Energy surged through them like waves on the ocean and beneath the dark illusion of wood and sawdust she could see the insubstantial outlines of pens and pencils, a stapler and a ruler.

Oliver hung up the phone. "Do you think," he asked the other two, "when Julia tucked her son in and told him good-night that last night, do you think she had any idea that it *was* the last time?"

Neither answered. The mood in the room became quiet and somber.

Donaldson was standing next to Julia, studying something in a file folder. Her true objective was so close. Her heart-shaped necklace in its evidence bag weighed down his breast pocket. She could see the bulge it made, even with just a superficial glance. She looked deeper and there it was, a faint outline wrapped in textured layers of shadow, floating above the framework of his skeleton and the complex, pulsing silhouettes of heart and lungs and the currents of blood flow. But she couldn't touch it, and as long as it remained in Donaldson's pocket she was as much his prisoner as she had been locked in his jail.

Chapter Eleven

Hunting High And Low

[A-Ha, 1985]

They came into Eugene from the northwest and Julia leaned forward, taking in all the changes to the city. She, John and Belle had all grown up here. She might have met her husband in kindergarten if he and his sister hadn't attended parochial school. In this familiar setting the trappings of the twenty-first century were more surreal than ever.

"What in the world is that?" she asked rhetorically. She looked at the signs sliding past and answered her own question. "That must be the Oregon Convention Center. They were building that last time I was here. I didn't realize it was going to look like that when it was done. That roofline looks like one of Madonna's bras."

She didn't know why they were here nor what they were doing. Donaldson was carrying her necklace; where he went, she went.

He made a right at Willamette Street. There had been a lot of changes since her last visit, mostly for the better. The beautiful old Tiffany building, damaged by fire, had been renovated, and both sides of the street were sprinkled with artwork. The old Ax Billy Department store was now an athletic club and there was an impressive structure of brick and glass off to the southwest, where Sears had been.

The streets themselves didn't seem to have changed much. They were headed toward John and Belle's old neighborhood. The senior Lodges had lived in the southern part of the city, not far from St. Ann's Catholic Church.

Donaldson took another right, turning off Willamette, and Julia perked up. If they continued on this street much farther, they were going to go right past her in-laws' house.

She leaned against the window, nose pressed against the glass, palm flat on the warm pane, and could only stare as they drove by the intersection.

The Lodges' had owned a two-story bungalow, one house from the corner. It hadn't been big or fancy, but it was neatly-maintained and the lawn was immaculate.

That house was gone now. Gone. The house, the garage, Muriel's canna lilies, and every blade of Edgar's perfectly-mown grass. The house on the corner was gone as well, and the one around the corner on the cross-street. The intersection had been widened and a big, new convenience store sat cater-corner on the larger lot created by the destruction of the three homes.

It had occurred to her that it might be--that it probably would be--different. Painted. Remodeled. She had never imagined that it simply would not be.

A pre-teen on a bike rode past on the sidewalk, followed by a lively collie. The dog gave her a wary, suspicious stare. The child didn't even notice her.

The church loomed before them, stately and elegant, the cemetery beautifully peaceful to one side. Donaldson pulled in and parked in the lot between a burgundy sedan and a flashy truck that was at least eight feet longer than any truck had a right to be. It had a back seat, for crying out loud. Donaldson got out and she slid after him. There was some kind of gathering going on at the church and Donaldson hovered in the gravel lot and studied the people moving on the east lawn. Julia, though, drawn by their proximity to the Lodge family plot, crossed the grass and came to a stop outside the cemetery.

On the other side of this fence there were probably two hundred bodies. But spirits other than Julia? None that she could see.

The fence was tall but the gate was low. With a self-conscious glance around--she *was* clad only in a nightshirt--she climbed over it. It was early afternoon. Short shadows around the tombstones were beginning to work their way to the east. Grasshoppers fled as she approached and when she passed a rocky, neglected corner at the back of the cemetery, an anxious killdeer tried to draw her off by faking a broken wing.

Julia had been here before. The Lodge's were an old-fashioned family, heavily invested in tradition. They'd been in Eugene since the 1800's, stolid, hardworking people who never quite made it. This plot was the only real inheritance they had and they attended it as religiously as they attended mass. Muriel checked it every Sunday afternoon, pulling weeds from around the headstones and putting out fresh flowers for holidays. Julia had helped her from time to time, trying, mostly in vain, to make peace.

They couldn't be entirely bad people. They'd raised John and Belle and *they* were wonderful.

She had to half circle a statue of an angel and duck between a cross and a stele to reach it. John's great-great grandfather's family were the first Lodges buried there. He and his wife and seven children. Three of the stones were tiny, with only a single date on them. One simply said "baby" and it always broke Julia's heart.

There were three new stones. The first was Edgar's and Julia didn't even know how she felt about that. She'd always felt that she bewildered him. He didn't know how to relate to her, or how to act in her presence. He'd confided once that he had a great-great-uncle who fought for the Confederacy. Another fought for the Union. They'd both died in combat and his own ancestor, the last of the family, had followed the Oregon Trail to escape the memories.

Julia didn't know if he was apologizing for his family history or blaming her for it. He didn't seem to know himself.

Edgar had died in the spring of 1996. Muriel, buried beneath the third stone, had hung around until late September of 2005. Julia pictured her aging like an apple, shrinking into a tough, shriveled, little ball, perpetually on the verge of rot.

Julia went to her knees in the grass before the center stone. A faint sheen of dust had settled on the marble face and her fingers did not disturb it, even as she felt the sharp edges of the letters carved there.

ANNABELLE MARY LODGE
APRIL 5, 1966 - FEBRUARY 13, 1987
SWEET JESUS HAVE MERCY ON HER SOUL

"Belle." she whispered. "Baby, what happened?" She tipped back her head and shouted at the sky. "Belle! Can you hear me? Sweetheart, where are you? It's Julia. BELLE? BEEELLLLLEEEE!"

A light breeze moved in a wave across the top of the grass and rustled through the fronds of the willow tree. Grasshoppers sang among the weeds that grew close around the bases of the headstones and the killdeer settled in her nest with her chicks. Julia's cry was lost like a dream on waking and no one and nothing answered her.

———♥———

When she pulled herself away from the cemetery and went in search of Donaldson she found him outside the side entrance that led into the church's community room. A standing sign advertised a fund raiser for a church-sponsored program for under-privileged kids. From the looks of things it was winding down. A couple of kids lingered, playing with an energetic puppy, while the adults took down flyers and folded the tables and chairs.

A young giant with broad shoulders and long dark hair left the room and headed towards the parking area. Donaldson straightened and stepped out into his line of sight.

"Volunteering with a charity. Nice. Or do you get paid for this gig?"

The young man stopped and drew himself up to his full height. "I volunteer," he said. "After all, I know what it's like to grow up without a father."

"Really? This is how you talk to your dad after all this time?"

"You're just a sperm donor. You were never my dad."

"And how lovely of your mother to turn you against me."

"You've never needed someone else to turn a person

against you."

Donaldson sighed. "Look, Kyle, I didn't come here to fight with you."

"I don't know why I'm even bothering to ask you this, but why did you come here?"

"I was hoping maybe we could make a fresh start. You're my son. I'd like to be in your life. Have a relationship with you."

"Now that I'm getting some attention for being a hockey player, you mean?" Kyle asked. "It's too little, too late. Whatever you want from me, I don't have any."

"I didn't ask you for anything," Donaldson said, a trace of annoyance creeping into his voice.

"You never gave me anything either," his son said. "No, wait. That's not quite true, is it? I do remember how you used to buy me coloring books and crayons and candy and soda pop. Anything to keep me occupied in the car so you could meet your side piece for a quickie when you were supposed to be taking me to the park."

"You did what?" Julia demanded. "You are such a sleaze ball."

"Well, I couldn't leave you with your mom," Donaldson said. "She was high."

Kyle stepped close, deliberately intimidating. "Mom had a lot of problems when I was a kid. I know that. But the biggest one of them all was you."

"She wants you to think that."

"Think that? *She* wants me to think that? I'm your son. I grew up with you, and I remember *everything*. I remember when you used me to cover up your affairs. I remember when you blew off my tenth birthday party to go out drinking with your friends and I remember when you showed up to my high school graduation drunk, with a stripper on your arm. I know you better than anybody and there is nothing--*nothing*--you can say to me that will change the way I feel about you one iota."

Kyle shouldered past Donaldson and resumed his path toward the parking lot.

"Even if I tell you that I'm the one who talked your

mother out of getting an abortion?" Donaldson called after him.

Kyle froze. "Not even that," he said.

"Because I *did*."

His son turned and met his eye. "I *know*."

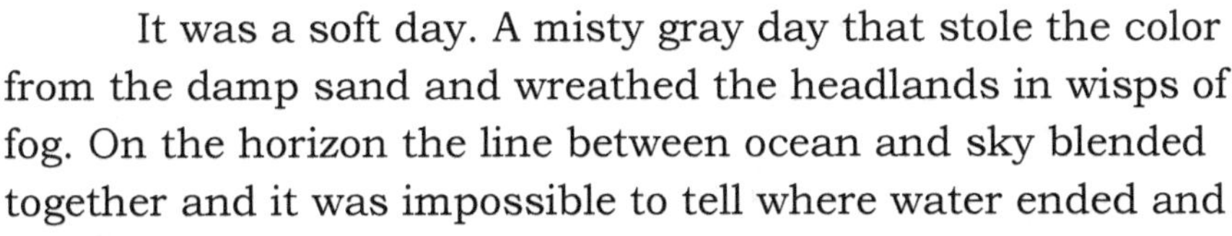

It was a soft day. A misty gray day that stole the color from the damp sand and wreathed the headlands in wisps of fog. On the horizon the line between ocean and sky blended together and it was impossible to tell where water ended and air began.

Donaldson took his suit coat off and tossed it to the side and settled down to sit on the beach. The mouth of Julia's cave loomed behind him, crime scene tape tattered and tossing in the breeze. A path up the side of the bluff suggested it hadn't been an effective deterrent to sightseers anyway.

Julia pulled her nightshirt down over her toes and settled near him, on the other side of his jacket. Her heart was in its usual pocket and she could almost see it, like looking into clouded water. She had learned to reach into the cloth as if she were putting her hand in the ocean, but she was no closer to picking it up than she had been when she first started.

Donaldson was in an odd, introspective mood. She suspected his encounter with his son had something to do with it.

His phone chimed and he answered it and Julia listened to his side of the conversation.

"Uh huh...uh huh...how'd he react?...Did he tell you anything new?...Huh. Color me not surprised...You record it?...Okay, send it to me. I'm following up a possible lead. I'll be back later. In the meantime, organize all the old recorded interviews. Transfer them from the cassette tapes to digital files so we don't lose them. We all need to listen to all of them again, see if we can pinpoint anything we might have missed the first time. Okay...Take care of it."

He hung up without bothering to say goodbye, flipped the phone around and tapped on its face. He set it on the ground between his feet and Julia moved closer when John's voice came from the device. The sound of it exacerbated her desire to be with him, the way the scent of food sharpened hunger. She thirsted for him.

"Deputy Min. Come in. What can I do for you? Here, have a seat. Would you like a cup of coffee?"

A door closed and a chair leg scraped across a floor.

"No thank you," Min said. "I just wanted to come tell you in person that the coroner has determined a cause of death for your wife."

"Oh."

The second year of their marriage John, loathe to miss work when he was trying so hard to make a good impression, had ignored a stomach ache that turned out to be an appendicitis. Julia had wound up rushing him to the emergency room in extreme pain in the middle of the night. His voice now sounded like it had then.

"What happened to her?"

"A sharp trauma to the base of her skull," Min said. "Initially we thought it was a gunshot wound but the medical examiner doesn't think so and we didn't find a bullet. We believe she was struck with something hard enough to puncture her skull and destroy the portion of her brain that controlled her bodily functions. Things like breathing and heartbeat. He says she'd have been rendered unconscious and died almost immediately."

"She didn't suffer?"

"Not so far as we can tell," Min said cautiously. "Not from the manner of her death, at any rate."

"But you have no way of knowing what might have been done to her while she was still alive," John said. "I understand. Believe me, my imagination has gone to that terrible place many times."

There was a long silence. It was Min who broke it.

"John, please tell me where you were and what you were doing the night that Julia disappeared."

"I can't. No. I can't. I'm sorry. It had nothing to do with Julia. I was nowhere near her. I wish I had been. But I wasn't and where I was has nothing to do with her death. That's all I can tell you. I'm sorry. Please don't ask me again."

"Donaldson isn't going to drop this. You know he's not."

"I know. But he's read me the Miranda many times and I also know that I have the right to remain silent."

"If you remain silent, people assume you're guilty."

He laughed, a short, sad sound that held no humor. "I'm used to that. Believe me."

"Will you tell me something else then?"

"Mmm. Maybe. What is it?"

"We have interviews on record with a lot of your coworkers. They said the company was small and tight-knit. They did a lot of things together outside of work, but you and Julia never participated. Why is that?"

"Oh, God." There was the light clink of a cup hitting a table and the brushing of fabric. "The guy I worked for, his name was Geoffrey Hunt. He owned the business. Had built it from the ground up. Considered it his own little kingdom. I was so happy when I got that damned job." He sighed. "We were always a blue-collar family. My dad was an auto mechanic. Most of my life we lived paycheck to paycheck. Old man Hunt offered me more money than I'd ever imagined I'd be able to make. I was the director of marketing. Good pay, benefits, retirement, a company car. I should have known it was too good to be true."

"How so?"

"Geoffrey Hunt was this wizened little old man, smiled all the time, looked like an elf in one of those cookie commercials."

"Yeah. And?"

"And he was the most racist person I've ever met."

It took Min a few seconds to respond. "Really?"

"Oh, yeah. He didn't meet my family until after he'd hired me. Julia thought he was this sweet little old man. She didn't know what he said to me after she'd gone home."

"What did he say?"

"He called her the N-word. I'm not going to say it. That word has never crossed my lips and it isn't going to now. You know the one I mean, though."

"Yeah. I know."

"He called her that. He said it was okay to keep one of them in the woodpile if you had to, but you weren't supposed to marry them."

"What did you do?"

"Nothing." John's voice was grieved. "I mean, I told him I didn't appreciate him speaking about my wife that way. But I didn't *do* anything. He just laughed and walked away and I went on working for him like nothing had happened. And I *shouldn't have*. I should have stood on principle. I should have defended the woman I love. I should have told him to go fuck himself--I'm sorry; forgive my language--and picked up my briefcase and never looked back. But I couldn't turn my back on all that money."

His laugh was bitter and a little mad.

"It wasn't a fortune in the grand scheme of things. But it was to me. We'd just bought a house. Jude was a baby and he needed so many things. I was afraid that if I quit that job I wouldn't be able to find another. I wouldn't be able to provide for my family. The man is supposed to be the breadwinner. I had that drilled into me from the minute I was born. It was my responsibility to be the breadwinner. And if I couldn't be the breadwinner, maybe Julia would come to her senses and real-ize she could do so much better than me. And then she'd leave me, like my parents always said she was going to."

Min spoke after a moment, her voice soft and hesitant. "I'm sorry."

"Don't be sorry for me," John said immediately. "Be disgusted with me. God knows, I am. Rose Meyers thinks Julia was wrong to fall in love with me and she was right. Because if I'd been a man of principle, if I'd quit that job like I should have done the minute he said that, I wouldn't have been able to afford to take them to the beach for a week every summer. She wouldn't have been there all alone that night when what-ever happened to her happened.

"This is why I accept that people think I killed her. Be-cause I didn't. But I'm as much responsible for her death as if I had.

Chapter Twelve

Total Eclipse of the Heart

[Bonnie Tyler, 1983]

Jude had changed in ways Julia hadn't even imagined. He'd taken after her father in physique and towered over her, nearly three times as tall as the little boy she remembered. His shoulders had broadened, his voice deepened into a rich baritone and his hair, black with just a hint of copper highlights, hung in loose curls to his shoulders. His eyes were the same--brown like hers but set in a face that was shaped like his father's.

If she'd been looking at a picture, she might not have known him, but when he walked into the sheriff's office her heart recognized her son.

The officer on the reception desk unlocked the door and ushered him back to the squad room.

"Julian Lodge," he told Min. "Donaldson wanted to see him?"

"Of course. Hello again, Jude. Donaldson's in his office. Just a second and I'll let him know you're here."

She left and Julia studied the man that her baby had become. He wore a dark suit in a good-quality material. His shoes were black leather, well-shined, and she wondered at the juxtaposition of business attire and long hair on a man. His tie was black with a discrete geometric pattern in vibrant shades of blue. It was tied in a Kelvin knot, the knot that his father had favored.

It had been Julia's own father who had taught her husband how to tie it. Growing up as a good Catholic boy, John had, of course, learned to tie the common half-Windsor that he'd worn to church every Sunday. It wasn't even something he thought about until he was out of school. Suddenly he was moving in unfamiliar social circles, acutely conscious of his blue-collar background and trying desperately to fit in. Rueben Meyers, unlike his wife, had taken a liking to his new son-in-law. He'd understood, without having to ask, the problems John was having, and he'd offered a solution.

Knowing and using different knots to tie his tie, he suggested, would send a subtle message to John's new associates that he was cultured and sophisticated. They'd spent a long Saturday afternoon with ties and open books on men's fashion scattered around the Meyers' living room; a breeze coming in the window and a Mariners game playing on the radio.

"Do you really think anyone's going to notice the knots in his tie?" she'd asked her dad later.

"How he looks isn't the point," he told her, looping an arm around her shoulders and dropping a kiss on her temple. "The point is how it makes him feel about himself."

Min returned, closing Donaldson's office door behind her.

"He's tied up right now. We just wanted to go over what you remember again. Take a new statement. in light of the developments in your mother's case. If you'd come with me, I can take care of that."

She picked up a file from her desk and led the way into a conference room, holding the door for Jude to follow her. Julia slipped in as well. It was a plain room, painted pale blue, with a chalkboard on the wall by the door and a single window overlooking the parking lot. A wooden table and half a dozen chairs took up most of the floor space. Jude pulled out a chair and sat down and Julia climbed up and sat on the table next to him, turned so she could see his face.

"Can I get you a cup of coffee?" Min asked.

"Yes, please."

"How do you take it?"

"Black, two sugars."

The young deputy left to get the coffee and Julia took

the opportunity to study her son. He was wearing a wedding ring and had an earring in his left ear. In the eighties a man wearing an earring in one ear was gay, but Julia couldn't remember which ear it was and she had no idea if it still carried that significance. She'd never imagined him being gay. Not that it mattered. He was her son. She'd love him no matter what.

His hands were smooth and free of calluses, his nails well-manicured and she could smell just a hint of cologne.

Min returned and set a Styrofoam cup down in front if him. She carried her own around the table and took a seat across from him.

"Thank you," Jude said, taking a sip.

"Thank you for coming in," Min countered. She folded her hands on top of the closed folder and looked him in the eye, her expression solemn and sad. "I realize this is coming thirty years late, but I wanted to tell you how sorry I am for your loss."

"Thank you," Jude said again.

She opened the folder and studied it for a moment. "You were very young when this happened, and I see that you weren't originally interviewed until several months later. I know this was all such a long time ago."

Jude stopped her. "You're talking about the day that defined my life. I've spent thirty years thinking about that day. Trying to sort out memories from things I might have only imagined. Figuring out what happened then and what happened at other times but just got mixed up with that day."

"Okay, well, why don't you just tell me in your own words, to the best of your recollection, what happened?"

Jude took another sip of coffee, pushed the cup aside and folded his own hands on the polished wood surface.

"I don't really have a cohesive memory. More like fragments, torn from the day. Some are still bright, others faded, some more tattered and frayed at the edges. Most of them are probably not even relevant."

"Just tell me everything. We'll sort them out later."

He tightened his mouth, tipped his head a bit to the right. "The first thing I remember is leaving the house that

morning. I always woke up early so I could tell my dad goodbye when he left for work. Usually I'd go back to sleep when he
was gone but that morning Mom got me dressed. She and Dad
loaded her car with stuff and she and I left the same time he
did."

"How did your parents seem then?" Min asked. "Did they
seem upset? Worried about anything?"

"No, they were happy. Cheerful. Teasing each other." He
looked directly at Min. "I know what Donaldson thinks. He's
wrong. My parents had a good marriage. They loved each other."

"Okay," she said easily. "I'm not saying they don't. I'm
just asking for details. We all just want to find out what happened. All right?"

Jude hesitated, then nodded reluctantly.

"What else do you remember?"

"We didn't stop for ice cream."

"Were you expecting to?"

"I'm not sure what I was expecting, or how much I understood. But I remember seeing the ice cream place and being
disappointed because we didn't stop. It was this little store,
on the way to the beach house. They made ice cream on site
and were known for their cherry floats. I remember standing
on tiptoe to peek through the glass into the ice cream case.
There were big, grey cardboard tubs of ice cream. The old lady
who worked there would let me sample them and she always
winked at me when she handed me my float."

"Yes, I think I know where you mean," Min said. "It's out
of business now but the building is still there."

"It was a ritual. We always stopped there first when we
went to the beach, but Mom didn't want to that day because it
was almost lunch time. She promised we'd go later, when Dad
was there. But, of course, we never did. We never did a lot of
things after that...." His voice trailed off.

He sat for a minute, staring off into the distance, and
Julia wanted to cry. She traced the outline of his jaw with one
finger. "Oh, sweetheart."

He cleared his throat and straightened. "I remember

playing beside the front stoop of the beach house while Mom unloaded the car. There was a flower bed there--more weeds than flowers, I suppose. The dirt was sandy and moist and I remember scooping it up between my hands and pressing it into fish shapes and little, crumbly mud pies."

"I hope you didn't try to eat them," Min said, teasing a small smile from him.

"Not so far as I recall. I believe, and I could be wrong about this, but I believe Mom served me canned ravioli and carrot sticks for lunch. With milk. We took a nap, or at least I did, and that afternoon we went looking for blackberries. We got lost in the woods above the beach and wandered onto the Millers' property."

She consulted her notes. "Right. Mr. Miller found you."

"Yeah. He wasn't too happy to see us there. There was a rattlesnake den in the rocks on the hillside and he said the hospital was a long way away if one of us were to get bitten. He walked us back down to the road to make sure we got there okay."

"And then what happened?"

"And then I was covered in blackberry juice. I swear, I'd eaten more than I'd put in the bowl. Mom let me paddle around in the shallows at the edge of the sand for a few minutes. Not long, of course. Even in August the water is cold. I had a hot bath and supper and it was time for bed."

Jude's eyes were distant, his tone introspective. "This I remember. I think I've been hanging onto this memory almost since it happened. With Dad not there, Mom let me sleep in the big bedroom with her that night." He closed his eyes. "I climbed into the bed, with the fresh, clean sheets and the fluffy pillows. Mom turned the light off before she joined me. The radio was turned on low and a light breeze came in the open window and seemed to carry the music. She climbed in behind me, pulled me against her and wrapped me in her arms. I can still smell the fabric softener in the sheets; the bath soap and the scent of her shampoo. There was no moon that night and the beach seemed to glow with a faint blue light. It reflected off the skin of her hand, making it stand out like a three-dimensional shadow against the pillow. She brushed the hair off my forehead and hummed along with the music and I fell asleep.

"When I woke up I was in a strange place. My mother was gone and I never saw her again."

Min let the silence settle over the room. She reached across the table and touched Jude's hand in sympathy and he gave her a slight, tired smile.

"When you woke up," she said, "was it light or dark outside?"

"It was daylight. The next day, at the Millers'. Charlie and Harriet were arguing about what to do with me. Charlie wanted to try to contact my family and Harriet said they should wait for someone to turn up. They were trying to keep it down, but I woke up anyway. The house smelled weird, like strange medicine and burned hair."

"Burned hair?" Min interrupted.

"That's what I thought at the time. In retrospect, I imagine it was pot smoke. I'd never smelled it so I had no frame of reference. And Charlie was fighting cancer at the time. Illness has a scent of its own. All I knew was that it was strange and I didn't feel well. I wanted my mother and she wasn't there. I cried and Charlie cried and tried to console me and eventually he took me back down to the beach house. He helped me get dressed and let me have pop tarts for breakfast. We were still there when my Dad showed up."

Min picked up her ink pen and doodled on the inside of the folder. "About your dad...how did he seem when he showed up that morning?"

Jude froze and gave her a hard look. "I don't remember."

"No? Nothing? He didn't seem angry? Or upset?"

"Of course he was upset. His wife was missing."

"But he didn't know that, supposedly, until after he arrived. How did he seem when he arrived?"

"I already know what Charlie Miller told you."

She glanced at her notes, but wasn't deterred. "I'm not asking you what Mr. Miller said. I'm asking you what you remember."

"Very little. I was upset. I wanted my mommy and daddy. When he showed up, I ran to him and he picked me up and held me. That's what I remember."

"Charlie said that he seemed tired, and his eyes were red, as if he'd been crying. Did you notice anything like that at all?"

Jude sighed, squeezed his eyes closed and pinched the bridge of his nose.

"Yes," he said finally, reluctantly. "Yes, he looked exhausted and I think he'd been crying. But it wasn't because he'd done something to my mother. He was absolutely bewildered that she wasn't there. He was stunned. And when her absence drew out and became a disappearance, when she continued to not be there in the days and weeks and months and years that followed, he was heartbroken.

"Listen. I don't know where he was that night or what he was doing. I don't know what his secret is nor why he's kept it for all these years. But my father is a *good* man."

Min closed the folder and looked him in the eyes. "Your grandmother doesn't agree," she said candidly.

"My grandmother isn't thinking clearly."

She frowned. "Would you say that to her face?"

"I would and I have. Do you have children, Deputy?"

"No, I don't. You do, yes?"

"I do, yes," he said, and even in the midst of this somber conversation a light burst in Julia's heart at the knowledge. "I have two. Daughters. Julia is seven and Lily's five." He leaned over the table, half rising from his seat with the fervor of his words. "My grandmother *lost* her daughter. I cannot fathom the pain that that entails. In her sorrow, she's lashing out and my dad makes a convenient target. But I grew up with him. I know him. I know him better than anyone and I will *never* not defend him and I will *never* believe that he would hurt my mother or anyone else."

He settled back into his seat, looking suddenly tired and older than his thirty-six years.

"We're all victims of my mother's murder," he said, "but in many ways my father is the most wounded of us all."

———❤———

Julia herself dwelled a lot on that last night, when she curled up next to her son for the last time and fell asleep. She could remember putting him to bed, turning on the radio and blowing out the vanilla scented candle. She'd lain beside him, between the cool, fresh sheets.

The last song she remembered hearing was That's What Friends Are For. Everything after that was a jumble--random sensations that might have been memories or dreams or only her imagination. She had a vague idea of violence. Of loud noise and quick pain and turbulence.

She had an impression of her own sodden corpse riding the storm surge, scraping through the underwater passage and thrusting out of the dark pool to be abandoned on the sand as the water retreated.

Chapter Thirteen

Young Guns

[Wham, 1983]

"I talked to an oceanographer with the university at Corvallis," Oliver said. "They've been mapping the ocean currents, trying to figure out where the body was dropped to wind up in the cave. They say it must have been between a mile and a mile and a quarter offshore and within half a mile of the cave, up or down the coast. Any further out and it would have been pulled away by the riptides and probably never recovered. Any closer and it would have washed ashore."

Donaldson and the two deputies were ensconced in his office, surrounded by boxes of files and piles of cartons labelled "evidence". What that evidence consisted of or where they'd gotten it, Julia had no idea.

"That gives us a strip a mile long and a quarter of a mile wide," Donaldson observed. "It doesn't really tell us much."

"It tells us that whoever dumped the body needed a boat."

"Yeah. But we already know that the Millers kept a small rowboat pulled up and turned over on the beach a hundred yards or so from the Lodge's beach house. Anyone could have taken it long enough to get rid of her."

"It would have had to be someone who knew how to handle a rowboat. And we know Julia was killed and dumped the night she disappeared. It was calm that night, but there was a big storm the next night. Anyone in a rowboat would have been swamped."

"She could have been dumped after the storm."

"Maybe, but unlikely," Oliver countered. "The scientists think it was the storm that pushed her body into the cave."

"How do they know it was that storm and not another storm? For all we know, Julia Lodge was held captive for months or even years before she was killed."

"You're just deliberately complicating this case," Oliver accused.

"You're just mad because you're trying to play Sherlock Holmes and I'm pointing out that you're more Lestrade. And not the reasonably competent Lestrade from the TV show, either. The dimwitted Lestrade from the books."

"Fine," Oliver growled.

A folding table was set up in one corner, with a couple of folding chairs to go with it. Min lifted a carton onto the table, sat down and started unpacking cassette tapes and file folders.

"I went to my parents for dinner last night," she ventured, carefully not looking up.

Donaldson gave her a predatory smile. "And what did the Min family have for Sunday dinner?" he asked. "Moo shoo gai shroom? Colonel Tso's fungus?"

Min rolled her eyes. "Pastrami on rye," she said.

"Oh. Well. Isn't that something?" He patted his pockets, then rifled through the papers on his desk.

"The thing is," she persisted, "they told me this rumor I thought you might be interested in."

"Hold that thought," Donaldson said, and wandered out of the room.

Min glanced up then and caught Oliver smirking at her.

"Pastrami on rye?" he asked softly.

"Korean barbecue and kimchee," she hissed. "Shut up. My mother makes amazing kimchee."

"Got leftovers?"

"Next time."

"I'll hold you to that."

Donaldson came back in looking at his phone.

"So I was saying," she tried again.

He looked up. "Were you? Oh right. You were about to

share some charming ethnic homily or something."

"I was going to tell you something that I think you might be interested in."

He dropped into his chair, set down his phone, folded his hands in front of him and gave her his attention. "By all means. Enlighten me."

"You remember I told you how my parents came here in 1990 and travelled up the coast following the mushroom crops?"

"Yeah. Sure."

"Well, when I was at their house last night we were talking about the Lodge case. Nothing confidential," she said hastily. "It's just that they'd seen the news about Julia's body being found and they were interested. They told me a story that was going around the pickers camps back in the early nineties. The rumor was that a mushroom hunter had found Julia Lodge's car."

Donaldson's eyes narrowed and his gaze sharpened. "Her car has never been recovered," he said.

"Yes, I know. But supposedly a few of the mushroom hunters knew where it is. The story is that they came across it hidden under brush in a ravine, somewhere along this stretch of coastline but a couple of miles inland."

"Then why didn't they report it?"

"Because it was on private land and they didn't have permission to hunt mushrooms there. They were afraid if they admitted they'd been trespassing they'd get arrested and be deported."

"Deported," he said. "For trespassing."

She lifted one shoulder. "I figure there's also a pretty good chance they weren't here legally. If the story's even true."

"If the story is true, how does that help us now? Do you know who these mushroom hunters were or where they supposedly found the car?"

"No," she said slowly, "but I've been thinking."

"A complicated pastime and one I'm not sure you're qualified to pursue, but by all means, continue."

Min swallowed a growl. "We know it was on a piece of

property with no houses nearby."

"How do we know that?"

"The mushroom hunters wouldn't have been brave enough to trespass if they'd thought someone might see them."

"Okay. Go on"

"We know that property can't have changed hands since 1986. The buyers would have certainly walked the ground and found the car."

"Unless the property owner was the killer and he or she passed it on to someone they could trust not to betray them."

"Okay, that's possible. But it's not a given and barring that possibility, it's likely the land hasn't changed hands. Or been built up, for that matter. There would have had to be, in 1986, a path the car could follow from the road to the ravine and since we know what kind of car we're looking for, we know how big the ravine would have to be to hide it."

"And what do you propose we do with this information?" Donaldson was truly listening now. Julia got the feeling he was impressed in spite of himself, not that he would tell Min that.

"We can use information on sales and ownership to narrow down the search parameters. There should be topographic maps of the area. If we could print one out on a transparency and get a Google Earth view of the same area at the same scale, we could pinpoint where to look, then enlarge it and search the satellite images for some signs of the car."

Donaldson leaned back in his chair, folded his hands across his stomach, and frowned.

"Not Google Earth," he said. "The images are too haphazard and don't come in close enough to see something that small. Go to the county assessor's office. They use aerial photography to assess property values. They'll have high-resolution shots of the whole county going back decades. Get pictures from the time Lodge disappeared as well as more recent ones. See if you can find pictures that were taken in the winter, when the foliage is thin."

Min stared at him. "You think it's a good idea?"

"Are you going or what?"

"I'm going! I'm going!" She jumped up and hurried from

the room. When the door had closed behind her, Oliver gave Donaldson a knowing look.

"It was a good idea, though," he said.

Donaldson sighed. "Fine. She can be a chubby, effeminate, Asian Watson for the day. But your ass is still Lestrade."

Chapter Fourteen

Purple Rain

[Prince and the Revolution, 1984]

Misty rain froze on the windshield in tiny droplets. They caught the red and blue police lights and refracted them across the dark highway, but birthed no rainbows. Julia scrambled across the console and followed Donaldson out into the frigid night. The cold drizzle plastered her thin sleep shirt to her skin and the pavement felt like ice beneath her bare feet. But she had discovered that a closed car reminded her too vividly of the cave and even Donaldson's dismal company was preferable to solitude.

A small car, of an indeterminate color in the low light, sat off the shoulder on the left, facing them. The front end was smashed in on the driver's side and the windshield spider webbed with cracks. A marked sheriff's car was already parked behind the wrecked vehicle, its headlights casting the smaller vehicle's doppelganger in shadow across the pavement. Within the darkness of that shadow lay the darker bulk of a fallen deer.

The air stank of burned rubber and blood and musk. Julia followed Donaldson past the animal. It was breathing, heaving deep, shuddering breaths. Donaldson skirted it without a glance, but Julia paused to look down at it with pity before she continued.

A pretty young blonde girl sat sobbing behind the wheel, her nose bloodied and makeup and tears smeared across her face. Deputy Oliver crouched next to her, holding her left hand in his own and talking to her in a soft voice.

"Whaddya got?" Donaldson demanded as he came up and Oliver's eyes rose to meet him.

"Deer strike," Oliver said.

"Yeah, no shit. You rolled an ambulance?"

Oliver patted the girl's hand, let go and stood so he could move away and speak to Donaldson privately. "I don't think she's hurt too bad, but her airbag didn't deploy and she smacked into the steering wheel pretty hard. And she's an animal lover, so she's practically hysterical about the deer."

"She drunk?"

"Nah. She blew a point-oh-one. We're just waiting for the ambulance and a tow truck." He drew his sidearm. "I'll go take care of the deer."

"No, wait." Donaldson wheeled back to the car and leaned over the door. "You like animals, huh?" he said to the woman.

She nodded, baring her teeth in a grim parody of a smile and fighting to talk through her tears. Her shoulders and voice shook with the words. "I killed it."

"I don't know. It's not dead yet."

"Sir," Oliver protested.

"No, really. Why don't you go get old lady Miller? You know where the Millers live? Up on the hill at the end of the coast road." He turned his attention back to the young woman. "She's something of a Dr. Doolittle. All the locals bring her wounded animals," he said, turning on a measure of charm Julia had never suspected him of possessing. She was highly skeptical of his motives for unveiling it now and so, by his expression, was Oliver.

Oliver took a flashlight from his belt and turned it on the deer. It lay across the white line, body twisted at an unnatural angle. When the light hit it, it moved its head feebly. Its chest was heaving.

"It's just suffering," Oliver said.

"What? You're a vet now?"

"I just think--"

"Well don't. You don't have the gift for it. Go."

The two men stared one another down. Oliver moved

first, touching the radio at his shoulder. "Dispatch, do you have an ETA on that ambulance?" He listened for a second. "Three minutes," he told Donaldson.

"I can handle this, Corporal," Donaldson said with a warning in his voice.

"Just thought you'd like to know when to expect company," Oliver returned evenly. He gave the woman a reassuring nod. "I'll be back as fast as possible," he said, and left with his lights and siren on.

As soon as he had gone, Donaldson crouched in his place by the open door and turned his full attention to the driver. "How ya doing? You gonna be okay? I don't think I caught your name."

"Megan. Megan Carter." Megan ran a hand across her face, trying to wipe away tears and only succeeding in smearing makeup and snot back into her hair.

"Megan. What a pretty name. Hi, Megan. I'm Manny. It's nice to meet you."

"You are such a sleaze," Julia said in disgust. "I can see why Oliver didn't want to leave her alone with you." She could hear the siren on the approaching ambulance and turned her attention to the deer.

It was a doe, she thought. It was big, at any rate, and had no horns. "Poor baby," she told it softly. "I'm so sorry." She had some idea of approaching it, trying to pet it or offer it some measure of comfort, but she stopped and backed away when it caught her in its gaze and moved its head, grunting softly and rolling its eyes in terror.

"It's okay, baby. It's okay. I'm not going to hurt you. Poor thing. It's all right. You're going to be fine. One way or another, you're going to be fine."

By the time Oliver returned with Harriet Miller, Megan had been taken away in an ambulance and a tow truck driver was loading her car on the back of a flatbed truck. Oliver parked on the opposite side of the road and Donaldson went to meet Harriet as she came around the car carrying a big black case that looked like an old-fashioned doctor's bag.

"So," he said brightly, "thanks for coming out." He gestured to the deer. "Poor thing got hit by a car. Think you can save it?"

"You *idiot*," she spat. "No, I can't save it. Its back is broken. I can see that from here. You should have let your deputy shoot it when he offered. How long did it take you to come get me?" she asked Oliver.

"About twenty-five minutes," he said after checking his watch.

"For twenty-five minutes you let this poor creature lie here and suffer unnecessarily," she accused Donaldson.

He shrugged, unaffected. "Hey, I'm not a vet."

"You don't have to be to have common sense and compassion."

"Do you want me to shoot it now?" Oliver asked, once more unholstering his sidearm.

"No, as long as I'm here I'll put it down. I can do it more gently, and save you a bullet and the reports that would go with using it.

She handed him her bag and went to the deer, circling it so that she came up behind its head and lowering herself awkwardly to the wet pavement. She was wearing sweat pants and what looked like a pajama top under a heavy cardigan. She took the deer's head into her lap gently, stroking its muzzle and talking softly to it.

Donaldson knelt in front of her, and spoke, his voice suddenly intense. "Tell me again about the night Julia Lodge left her son at your house."

"I already told you about that." She directed her next words to Oliver. "You can play nurse. Look in my bag."

"What do you need?" he asked, opening it. "Chloroform?"

"No. The movies get that wrong, you know. It takes twenty or thirty minutes to knock someone out with chloroform. This poor baby's suffered enough. There's a thing in there that looks like a handgun."

"The man with Julia," Donaldson persisted. "Was it John Lodge?"

"What is this thing?" Oliver asked curiously, finding the item and handing it over

"Knacker gun. Vets use it to put down large animals. It delivers a blow to the temple that will knock her unconscious, then I'll open a vein in her throat and let her bleed out." She positioned the barrel of the weapon against the side of the animal's head.

Donaldson leaned in close. "Tell me, Harriet. Charlie's not here to hear what you say. He doesn't even have to know that we talked."

She gave him an incredulous look. "You think that I'm *afraid* of *Charlie*?" She punctuated her disgust by pulling the trigger on the knacker gun. It had a report not unlike a .22. The deer jerked and went limp. Blood spilled from its nose and trickled from its mouth and ear. "There's a scalpel in there. I'll need that next," she told Oliver, handing him back the gun.

"I can tell you want to tell me something. And I can tell that Charlie doesn't want you to. What else am I supposed to think?"

"Well you just let me tell you something, mister." Harriet moved the deer's head to the edge of her knee, shifting and angling it so the blood would run downhill, away from her and, perhaps not coincidentally, towards Donaldson's shoes. "Charlie Miller is the kindest, most gentle person you'll ever meet." She took the scalpel Oliver offered her and drew it swiftly across the deer's throat. Blood gushed, mingled with the increasingly icy rain and ran in pink rivulets down the asphalt.

"He was sent to Vietnam, you know? He was just a boy. He saw terrible things. He was captured by the Viet Cong and they were *barbarous*. He came home and got spit on and called a baby killer by the very people he'd been serving for. He's had cancer *three times*. That man has seen more hardship than any ten people had ever ought to. But he never let it harden him. He never let it make him mean."

Steam rose from the deer's warm blood, and something else. A thin tendril of something luminous, barely substantial but definitely there. It rose with the mist and puddled in the air above the dying animal. The three living beings ignored it, but Julia watched, fascinated, as it took the form of a sleeping deer.

"And you, sir? You're not fit to clean his boots."

"I'm not offering to clean his boots. I just want you to tell me what happened the night that Julia Lodge disappeared."

The dying deer struggled feebly; even unconscious it was reluctant to release its hold on life. Its muscles twitched and its chest heaved with desperate gasps. Its spectral double remained perfectly still, but the luminescence faded and color began to fill in. First it developed a spotted coat, like a fawn, but the brown spots grew and bled together until it was identical with the deer below it.

"You're a horrible person."

"Probably," Donaldson conceded easily. "What about Julia Lodge? Was she a horrible person?"

"What? No. Of course not."

"What was she like then?"

"Like? Well...she was lovely, I suppose."

"You suppose?"

"I didn't know her well, but she seemed a sweet little thing. A good mother, I'm sure of that. You could see how much she loved her son."

"Her poor son," Donaldson persisted, "who had to grow up without her. Don't you want to help me punish the person responsible for that? Don't you want to help me catch her killer?"

The deer on the ground gave a last gasp and its chest stilled. The misty, silver tendril connecting the two does parted and the floating deer--the deer spirit? The astral deer?--took a breath and twitched. A strange, rich glow surrounded them, tinting the droplets of water as they fell from the sky.

Purple rain, Julia thought, and wondered if somehow Prince had known.

The astral deer started moving, feebly at first but then with increasing purpose. It heaved itself up and stood, like a newborn, on trembling legs, looking around itself.

"Hi, there, baby," Julia said gently.

The deer saw her. Its eyes widened and its nostrils flared and it turned away from her and bolted. A beautiful and brilliant white glow opened up in front of it. The deer ran into it and the light snapped out of existence behind it with an electric crackle. In its wake it left only darkness and the scent of ozone.

"Tell me," Donaldson insisted. "One question. Yes or no. Was John Lodge the man who was with Julia the night she disappeared?"

Harriet reached a hand up. Oliver caught it and hauled her to her feet while Donaldson scrambled up as well. She took her bag back and turned to face him, clasping it in front of her in both hands, like a shield.

"It certainly looked like him to me," she said.

———♥———

The stone Donaldson was carrying in his pocket was not the first heart pendant Julia had worn around her neck.

The summer she was seven her parents took her on a long vacation. They'd driven north to Portland, then followed highway 30 along the Columbia River to Astoria and returned home on the coastal highway. They'd eaten in truck stops and diners and hole-in-the-wall cafes and spent the nights in whatever motels they'd happened to find, searching the passing scenery for lighted vacancy signs against a purple twilight sky. The trip had been one of the high points of her childhood.

She remembered Portland; the zoo and the botanical gardens. She'd gotten a charm bracelet from the gift shop at the children's museum and her dad had used his brand new Kodak Instamatic camera to take pictures of her and her mother among the flowers at the International Rose Test Gardens.

And she remembered the long hours in the back seat of her parents' big Oldsmobile, winding along two-lane highways through the summer mountains. She was wearing shorts and her mother had put a folded beach towel on the seat to protect the back of her legs from the hot plastic. None of them wore seatbelts and as they took the curves she slipped and slid from side to side. Air conditioning meant driving with all four windows down. She had a book with her, a new Trixie Belden as she recalled, with a stiff, glossy cover and the worst excuse for glue along the spine. She tried to read but the wind caught at the pages and tore them out wholesale. Her mystery, loose and disarrayed, lay scattered all over the car. She was sure there was at least a chapter lost along the river.

Her dad's big hands were sure on the wheel. His head was full of poetry and as they travelled through the forests and along the coast he'd recited passages from Keats and Browning, From Frost and Gwendolyn Butler and Emily Dickenson, Longfellow and Emerson and Alfred Lord Tennyson.

The thing she remembered the most about that trip, though, was a nondescript little gas station and souvenir shop in some long-forgotten beach town. It might have been Waldport, for all she knew. The shop might even have been Zoosie's, where she and her husband bought ice cream floats every August, though if it was it had changed enough that she couldn't recognize it for sure.

They'd stopped for gas and to use the restroom. It was a long, low building on a gravel lot, set against the background of the ocean receding into the sky. Julia and her mother waited for her father to pay the attendant for the gas and they'd entered the building together, cautious. This was strange territory and you never knew how Black folks were going to be received. The interior was dark and it took a minute for her eyes to adjust.

The heart pendant had been the last one in a cardboard display case sitting atop a glass counter that held tubs of ice cream. The shop was full of touristy memorabilia--racks of picture postcards, ceramic thimbles with the Oregon state seal, collectible spoons and shot glasses and chunks of pumice set in decorative cubes. But the heart had caught her attention at once, as if it were calling out to her.

It was just a cheap piece of junk jewelry, designed to appeal to little girls like her, but she thought it was the most beautiful thing she'd ever seen. It was cut glass, faceted like a diamond, and when she found a sunbeam coming in a dusty window and held it up to the light, it shone with a brilliant radiance that was at once, somehow, both white and every color she could imagine.

It came with a flimsy chain and her doting father bought it for her and fastened it around her neck the first time himself.

She wore it for years, eventually replacing the chain with a better one. She'd taken it off for the last time the day of her daddy's funeral.

He'd had a massive heart attack and they'd known it was bad, but she never really believed he'd die. He couldn't *die.* He was *Dad.* But he had, while she slept on John's chest in a chair in the Intensive Care waiting room. He'd eschewed Dylan Thomas' famous entreaty and gone, ever so gently, into that good night.

She'd stood beside the coffin and taken off her necklace, tucked it into the palm of his right hand, kissed his forehead and turned away.

That had been less than two years before her own fatal August and she'd never really gotten over it. She would still, from time to time, break down in unexpected tears at the knowledge that his kind spirit had fled. His beloved body was in the ground.

Even now, now that she was herself on this side of mortality, she was bereft by his absence. She wondered where he was and why he didn't come for her. And she wondered if, somehow, her own soul had known something her consciousness wasn't privy to.

Because the light that had come to collect the spectral deer was familiar to her. It was stronger and larger and infinitely more powerful and more pure, but it was familiar. It was that same beautiful and brilliant illumination that had shone up at her from the depths of her glass heart.

Chapter Fifteen

Like A Prayer

[Madonna, 1989]

"Bring your toys to work day?"

Oliver grimaced under Donaldson's snide tone but set the action figure carefully on the edge of his desk. "Did you see the news last night? Columbus, Ohio?"

"The cop that was killed?" Min asked. "I saw that. That was horrible."

"Part of the job," Donaldson said, not looking up from the folder he was studying.

"We had the news on during dinner and my kids saw it. Kyle was pretty freaked out. He decided to send Mikey to work with me, to 'have my back.'"

Donaldson frowned at him. "That's the stupidest thing I've ever heard."

Oliver bristled. "Well I'm sorry. My kids love me. I realize that's not something you have experience with."

"Asshole." Donaldson turned on his heel, strode into his office and slammed the door.

"Well I think it's sweet," Min said.

"Sweet," Julia echoed. "Yeah. Sweet. And freaky." She leaned down, putting her eyes at the level of the bright plastic figurine. "Of all the things to make it into the twenty-first century..."

———❤———

"Wait. Wait, wait! They're what?"

Early sunlight filtered through the leaves of the lilac bush outside the window, caught the ever-present crystal pendant between Belle's breasts and scattered tiny rainbows around the darkened living room. She was curled up on one end of the couch, still in her sleep shirt, ensconced in a nest of schoolbooks and note paper with her open Trapper Keeper on the cushion beside her.

She let her notebook slide to the side and Julia caught a glimpse of a hand-drawn picture of a squid, carefully labeled and surrounded by notes. Belle was barefoot with her hair hanging loose around her face and a mark left by a wrinkle in her pillowcase not yet faded from her cheek.

The house was a mess, with toys scattered across the floor and pages from the morning paper covering the dining table, but Julia didn't care. She was settled in her own favorite chair, wrapped in a bathrobe and with her hair still wet. She had a copy of The Hitchhikers Guide To The Galaxy in her lap, her right index finger marking her spot.

"They're turtles," John said. He and Jude were lying on the floor watching cartoons. Jude lay on his stomach with a cereal bowl on the carpet in front of him. A few bright circles floated in milk gone gray from the mixture of complimentary colors leached into it.

"Mutant turtles," Julia clarified.

"But they're teenagers," Belle said slowly. "And ninjas?"

"That's about the size of it."

"Oh my *god!* That is like totally the most bizarre thing I've ever heard. Who comes up with this stuff?"

John kicked one foot up off the floor and smacked it lightly into the side of her leg. "Don't be dissing our turtles, y'doof."

"Doof?" she said. "Doof! Who you calling a doof, you doof? Look at you." John was still in his pajamas, with his chin resting on his left fist and a toy van clutched in his right. "What does Julia even see in you?"

"That I'll never know," he said, his voice a bit too serious for Julia's liking.

She studied him thoughtfully. "He has a nice butt," she confided in her sister-in-law. "I'm really very fond of that butt."

John turned his head to shoot her a grin over his right shoulder, his face bright red. Both the Lodge siblings were fair.

It was ridiculous how easily she could make them blush.

He turned back to his cartoon and the high color faded but, Julia noticed, the back of his neck and the tip of his ear remained an angry pink. She narrowed her eyes.

"When did you get a sunburn?"

John dropped the toy and slapped a hand to the back of his neck. "Ah, it's nothing."

"Okay, that's good. But that's not what I asked you. I thought you were working late all week. When did you have time to get a sunburn?"

"Oh. I, uh..."

Belle was focused on her notebook, eyes wide, worrying her bottom lip with her pen. Julia switched her attention to her. The girl was constitutionally unable to lie.

"Annabelle, when did your brother get a sunburn?"

Belle frowned and raised her eyebrows, not looking at John. "Maybe when he was doing yard work for Mom yesterday."

"I just went by on my lunch hour," he said. "The grass was getting a little long and Pop shouldn't have to worry about it. He works an actual job, after all, while all I do is sit behind a desk all day."

"Now that's funny," Julia said sourly. "It's your mouth moving but I hear your momma's voice coming out." Her father-in-law managed a grungy little service station that catered mainly to logging trucks. That industry was in serious decline and business was slow, as he made sure to tell everyone. Every time Julia had been to see him at work he'd been holed up in the office, sitting on a ratty old couch drinking soda pop, watching soap operas and game shows on a black and white TV.

"Our yard is getting long too. I know." The muscles of John's shoulders bunched as he pushed himself up to all fours. "You know what? I can just go –"

"No, don't be stupid." Julia kicked him lightly with the tip of her bare foot. "I'm not worried about the yard. I just...I hate the way your mom manipulates you."

"She's my mom. They're my parents. I should do things

for them."

"You do a lot for them. They should appreciate you more." She put her book down, no longer in the mood to read, and sighed. "I hate it when you hide things from me. It makes me feel like you don't trust me."

He sat up and turned around, leaning towards her and looking her in the eye. "Of course I trust you. I was just trying to avoid conflict. You and Mom don't exactly get along very well."

"Well... you should have come and got me. Maybe I could have weeded the flower beds for brownie points. I am willing to *try* to play nice, you know."

"It probably wouldn't have been a good time for it," he said. "She's in a mood right now."

"When is she not?" Julia held up a hand, palm out. "Sorry. Sorry."

"Is it my fault?" Belle asked. "She wants me to come home but I'm avoiding it because she's got this guy she's trying to set me up with."

"It's not you," John reassured her. "You heard about Timmy Woolwright?"

"Oh. Yeah."

"Timmy Woolwright?" Julia asked.

"A boy from our church. A few years younger than Belle," John said. "He killed himself last week."

"Oh, God. I'm so sorry. Was your mother very close to him?"

John and Belle exchanged a glance and in that fraction of a second Julia knew that it would be Belle who answered her and understood why. While John understood and reluctantly acknowledged his parents shortcomings, it obviously hurt him to do so. It was as if their failures were in some respect his fault, and he avoided saying or doing anything that would cast one of them in an unflattering light. Belle, growing away from them as she gained her independence, was less reticent.

"She wasn't close to him. It's not his death she cares about."

"I'm sure she cares about it," John objected. "She's not a monster."

"They're giving him a funeral mass. Burying him in the church cemetery. He'll be the first suicide victim buried in our cemetery since the Vatican changed the rules."

"Oh, right. Vatican two?" John and Belle had been trying to explain to her the complicated politics of their faith.

"No. Vatican two was a long time ago, before I was born. When John was a baby. This was just a couple of years ago."

"The church stance on suicide hasn't changed," John said. "It's still considered a mortal sin. But we recognize that there can be extenuating circumstances, like mental illness or the fear of suffering. Refusing someone a funeral mass or refusing to bury them in hallowed ground is presuming a judgement that only God can pass. And it's denying their family the comfort of hope. So the Vatican has given permission for priests and bishops to allow services for suicides, at their discretion."

"And your momma's not happy."

The second Vatican council, as Julia understood, had been intended to help the ancient institution fit more comfortably in the modern era. The changes they had handed down seemed commonsense to Julia. Trivial, even. Priests had been given permission to face the celebrants rather than the altar and translate the mass into English, for example. But some Catholics still resented it bitterly, and none more bitterly than Julia's mother-in-law.

"I talked to Sister Jude about Timmy," Belle said.

Sister Jude was an elderly nun who had been a champion for and confidante of both the Lodge siblings. That John and Julia's son's nickname was Jude was not a coincidence.

"What did she say?"

"We prayed for him. I can't imagine being so lost and alone and desperate that the only solution you can see is to end your life."

———❤———

Julia slid down to sit on the floor, her back to Oliver's desk and the Ninja Turtle action figure above her head.

"That was in the spring of '85. Sister Jude and I were the only two people, I think, who ever stood up for John or Belle. She had an aneurysm that October and died in her sleep. Without me, they wouldn't have had anyone."

Chapter Sixteen

Fame

[Irene Cara, 1980]

"Which camera am I talking to?"

"Don't worry about the cameras, please. Just talk to me."

The television studio was smaller than Julia would have expected and the set at one end of it was simple. A pair of matching, royal-blue armchairs sat, angled towards one another, against a wall decorated with a stylized city skyline. The wall held a large video screen and a logo at one side read, "Crime Watch Northwest with Tori LeGrande." Donaldson sat in the chair on the left and Tori sat in the other.

She was a slender young woman in her mid twenties, close to the age Julia had been, dressed in a tailored pantsuit with conservative jewelry and long, auburn hair swept up into an elegant knot at the nape of her neck. Julia was accustomed to female celebrities in tight, short skirts and blouses with low-cut necklines and padded shoulders. Big hair and dramatic makeup and bouncy personalities. The wheel of fashion had turned. Tori was more Katherine Hepburn than Kate Jackson.

Multiple lighting rigs turned the set into a bright oasis. The equipment was like something out of Star Trek. Julia lurked in the shadows behind the cameras, fascinated but not by changing fashions nor technological advances.

She was not the only one who was there in spirit only.

"I like to mess with the cameramen," the old man said. "The redhead smokes medicinal marijuana. He can see me sometimes afterwards but nobody believes him because he's high."

"Medicinal marijuana," Julia echoed. "Is that what he's planning to tell the cops?"

"No really. It's a thing now."

"Huh. Well, cool beans."

Julia's picture had appeared on the wall screen. A lighted sign that said, "on air" flashed on and Tori faced one of the cameras and spoke to it directly.

"Sometime during the overnight hours of August 7th and 8th, 1986, 26-year-old Julia Lodge left her young son with a neighbor couple she barely knew and disappeared with a man they could not conclusively identify. Despite an intensive, nationwide search, no trace of her was ever found. Not, that is, until last July, when a teenage boy, exploring a newly-opened cave less than a mile from the beach cottage she was renting, discovered her skeletal remains. Her cause of death? Murder. I'm Tori LeGrande and this is Crimewatch Northwest."

She indicated Donaldson. Julia was standing beside one of the cameras. It had a screen attached to the eyepiece that showed what it was filming in real time. His face appeared on it in 3/4 profile. "We have with us this evening the lead investigator on the case, Detective Manfred Donaldson, of the Lincoln County, Oregon, sheriff's department." She turned to him. "You've been investigating this case for a long time. Would you like to tell us about it?"

Julia looked away. "So why are you hanging around a television studio?"

"My little girl is the stage manager. That's her, over by the monitor there." He'd introduced himself as Eli Thrasher. He was, or had been, in his early eighties. Fluffy white hair accentuated the pink of his chin and cheeks and worry lines creased his forehead. Like Rex, he was interacting with the physical realm.

He slapped at one of the cables dangling from the nearest camera and it swung back and forth, brushing against the cameraman's leg. The cameraman glanced down at it, eyes wide. A muscle jumped in his cheek and he resolutely turned back to the stage.

"...that for more than thirty years he has stood on his right to remain silent."

"And you've never charged him?" Tori asked.

"I've never had a strong enough case. Until this summer, I've never even been able to prove conclusively that Julia was the victim of foul play. I've always known that she was. But I've never been able to prove it. But somewhere out there, maybe even watching this show, there is someone who knows something who can help me finally bring this man to justice."

"So your husband killed you, huh?" Eli asked. "That's rough. I feel you, as the kids say."

"My husband didn't kill me."

"Oh? Who did?"

"I don't know." Julia clenched her fists, frustrated. "But it wasn't John. I know John. He loved me. He'd never hurt me."

"You don't know. So, a stranger?"

"Yes? I don't know. I don't remember. I just...I woke up dead."

"So it could have been your husband."

"No! I know him!"

"Huh. Maybe. Do you know why I didn't go into the light when I died?"

On the soundstage Tori told the audience that they'd be right back. The "on air" light clicked off and the crew relaxed.

"No, why didn't you?" Julia asked.

"I decided to wait for my wife. Bea. We were married for 52 years."

"Oh. That's sweet."

"Yeah. Not so much." He fell silent. She glanced over and found him watching her seriously. In his wrinkled old face his gray eyes were disconcertingly young. "I thought she loved me too."

"I'm sorry?"

"I'm not waiting for her out of affection. I'm waiting to confront her. My wife murdered me. I want to look her in the face and ask her why."

Julia took a moment to digest this. The commercial break had ended and Tori and Donaldson were quietly watching the monitor behind them as it played a reenactment of the last day of Julia's life.

"Are you...I'm sorry, but--"

"Am I sure?" Eli asked. "I was there, you know."

"Yeah, but. You were probably busy dying and all. And if you were married 52 years, she must have been pretty elderly herself."

"I'm not saying she stabbed me to death," he said. "Hell, if she'd done that, maybe she'd have gotten caught." He sighed. "I had a stroke, right? Partially paralyzed, couldn't get around too well. She had to take care of me and it wasn't any fun. I get that. But you take care of people you love. I took care of her and the kids all those years. I worked my fingers to the bone putting a roof over her head and food on the table. Flowers every Valentine's Day. Two weeks vacation every summer. The beach. The mountains. The Grand Canyon. Disneyland."

"...but I knew it was her as soon as I saw the skeleton," Donaldson was saying. "I knew it here." He touched his chest. "And then, when I started examining her remains, the first thing I found, half sticking out of the sand as if she were beckoning to me with it, I found this." He held up Julia's necklace and the camera near her zoomed in and focused on it.

"What happened?" Julia asked Eli. "She killed you by not taking care of you? Is that what you think?"

"She killed me by grinding up several of my heart pills into my orange juice, so that I overdosed on them."

"She made it look like you killed yourself?"

"Oh, no! No. That would have invalidated my life insurance. No, she planned this all out in advance. Convinced everyone that the medicine I was on was making me absent-minded. Hell. She even convinced me of that. Brought me food she said I'd asked her for, even though I didn't remember doing so. Pretended we were in the middle of conversations and I'd just stopped talking. She even asked the doctor about it. Told the kids how worried she was because I kept forgetting mundane things, like taking my pills. She did apologize, kind of, when I was dead. She said she'd waited too long to enjoy herself to spend the rest of her life nursing me. And then she rinsed out the glass and turned on the waterworks before she called 911.”

"I'm sorry," Julia said.

"I get her not wanting to take care of me. I get that, okay? But she could have asked the kids for help, couldn't she?" His voice had turned plaintive and he was looking not at her but at the woman he'd identified as his daughter. "They'd have taken me. They're my kids. They loved me. I mean, they must have loved me. Didn't they?"

"Yes. Of course." What else could she say?

The TV segment was wrapping up with a final statement from Donaldson. "...but I do know one thing. Julia Lodge's sweet soul is crying out every day for justice. Fortunately," he found the camera he'd been seeking earlier and looked directly into it, "justice is my business."

———♥———

It was raining, as it so often did in the Great Northwest, and the city had doubled. Every lighted window and neon sign cast a bright, silent ghost of itself across the wet pavement.

Julia gazed down, seeking in vain her own reflection. It seemed as if she was looking into another Oregon, the Oregon of her heart and memories. It beckoned her, tantalizingly close and forever out of reach.

The shower picked up strength. A wind came up and Donaldson swore and clicked open his car and she had to leave both Portlands behind and slip into the vehicle before he drove off without her again.

Chapter Seventeen

All Out Of Love

[Air Supply, 1980]

"I'm going to record this interview, do you understand?"

The cassette in the dusty old machine stuttered. Min smacked it on the side and it smoothed out and continued to roll the tape from spool to spool. The plan to transfer the tapes to modern media has fallen through for technical reasons Julia didn't understand. Watching the young woman figure out how to work a simple cassette player had been entertaining.

Julia perched in a wooden chair across the desk from the young deputy. She wanted to hear this, but was wary of draining the battery by her very presence.

"Okay." Belle's voice was thin and quavery.

Her mother's was not. "Hold *still*, Belle. Do you want me to stick a pin in your leg?"

"No, ma'am." Her voice was quiet. To Julia's ear it was sad and hopeless and it was not lost on her that this interview had been recorded less than twelve hours before she'd chosen to end her own life.

"I'm investigating the disappearance of your sister-in-law, Julia Lodge." Donaldson sounded younger. Three decades of use and whiskey had textured his voice.

"I don't see why." That was Muriel Lodge again, as cranky and quarrelsome as ever. "Good riddance to bad rubbish, that's what I say."

"Momma!"

"Hold *still*, Belle. I'm going to the trouble to make you this pretty dress. The least you can do is hold still while I pin up the hem. Do you *want* to get married in a dress with a crooked hem?"

"No, ma'am."

Donaldson sighed. "Your brother says he hasn't seen or heard from his wife since August the 7th, when she left Portland for a vacation rental in Waldport," he said. "Have you seen or spoken to her since then?"

"No." The word was barely a whisper, followed by a tiny hiccup.

"She's crying," Julia told Min, wishing the young deputy could hear her. "Can you tell? She's crying."

"Do you have any idea what happened to her or where she is now?"

"I think we all know what happened to the girl," Muriel said.

"You old bat," Julia said. "You don't know anything."

"You have a theory?" Donaldson asked.

"Obviously, she decided she was tired of being a wife and a mother and left my boy and his son behind for greener pastures. His father warned him about this. The first time he brought her home, her in her designer clothes and fancy jewelry."

"Designer clothes?" Julia echoed incredulously. "Fancy jewelry? I shopped at the mall. I got most of my jewelry at craft fairs. You really had to stretch to find things to criticize me for, didn't you?"

"What do you mean, warned him?" Donaldson asked.

"That she was in it for the money. Obviously, she was trying to attract a sugar daddy. We told him, he's just not ever going to be rich enough to keep a woman of *that* sort. Of course, by then it was already too late. She'd seduced him with her flashy looks and loose morals. He'd given in to her."

"Given in to her."

"Men are weak, young man. We don't hold it against you. God has given you certain appetites. It's only natural for you to take what's offered, if you know what I mean. That's why young women must be chaste and proper."

"She didn't leave," Belle's tears were obvious now.

"She wouldn't leave. She loved John and she loved Jude. She wouldn't just disappear. Something happened to her. Something bad."

"Well, if it did, I expect she deserved it," Muriel said, self-satisfied. "Bad things happen to bad girls, you know."

Julia growled and put her hand down on top of the tape recorder. Energy seeped out of the batteries giving her a burst of strength and a taste of copper. The tape wound to a stop as the machine died.

Min smacked it again and growled herself when nothing happened this time.

"Man," she said to the empty room. "That old broad was a piece of work."

"Sweetheart," Julia said, "you don't know the half of it." She laughed, half amused as a memory floated to the surface. "You should have been there when we told her we were getting married."

———♥———

The Lodge house was always dark. Dark wallpaper and dark carpet were interrupted only by the deep honey finish of the highly polished hardwood trim. Tea-dyed lace doilies topped the backs of immaculate imitation Queen Anne furniture protected under plastic dust covers. Heavy drapes cut off any stray sunbeams and floor lamps and desk lamps with harvest gold shades cast shadows across the high, off-white plaster ceilings.

Julia had wondered, more than once, how two children as bright as John and Belle could have grown up in such a place. She'd mentioned it to John once.

They were talking about Belle. It was while they were trying to find scholarships and grants to help her pay for college. In Julia's eyes "bright" also applied as much, if not more, to John. She knew he didn't think so. It was a constant source of frustration to her, the way he undervalued himself.

"Where would God send light but into darkness?" he'd asked. "He knew we needed--that *I* needed--her brightness."

She didn't share his faith but she respected it, so she'd just shaken her head and let it go. It was on a Sunday, as it happened, that they'd braved the lion's den with news they'd both known wouldn't be welcome.

They'd gone to church with Belle and the elder Lodges and afterwards his parents hadn't been able to easily refuse him when he brought her home for Sunday dinner. John and his father had retired to the living room to read the paper and discuss the news and Julia had followed Belle and her mother into the kitchen. Determined to show willing, she'd offered to help with dinner.

"Oh, how sweet of you," Muriel Lodge said. Her tone vibrated with an underlying frisson of horror and her brittle smile completely failed to contradict the dismay in her eyes. "I do think Belle and I have everything under control. I get up early on Sundays and bake bread and there's a roast in the Crock Pot and salad in the refrigerator." She hesitated, then moved to the sink, staring at Julia meaningfully. "We always wash our hands before we eat," she prompted, doing so ostentatiously.

Julia tucked her tongue into her left cheek and regarded her drily.

"That's funny," she said. "We usually just take off our shoes and pick the knife and fork up with our toes."

Belle made a strangled noise and turned away, her shoulders shaking.

Muriel stared at her in dismay, mouth open. Julia gave her a saccharine smile, moved past her to wash her own hands, then picked up the stack of dishes Muriel had set out on the counter. "I'll just set the table, shall I?"

It never really got better than that. Edgar sat at one end of the table. ("John's father sits at the *head* of the table. It's his *right* as the *head* of the *household*.") Muriel sat at the other. John was seated at his father's right with Belle across from him and Julia between Belle and Muriel, as far from John as the small table allowed. The meal itself was much like the house. It looked like a photo from Better Homes And Gardens but it lacked substance in the real world. The bread was dry, the meat tough and the vegetables overdone.

Muriel asked Edgar how his work week had gone and he

filled the uncomfortable silence with a gruff monologue about brake jobs and oil changes sprinkled with mundane gossip concerning people Julia had never heard of before. It wasn't until Muriel and Belle had brought in desert--sticky angel food cake topped with glazed fruit--that Muriel asked her children if either of them had something they'd like to share.

"I've been invited to join the chess club," Belle said shyly, her cheeks pink with suppressed pleasure.

"Way to go, shrimp!" John cheered. He reached across the table to give her a high-five and she beamed at him.

"Belle!" Julia said, "that's wonderful! You'll have so much fun!"

"I'm not so sure," Muriel said cautiously. "You're trying to attract a husband, dear. Boys don't like smart girls. They intimidate them."

"The best boys love smart girls," Julia disagreed and Muriel glared at her.

"We'll talk about it later."

"But, Momma--"

"I said later, Annabelle. Now it's your brother's turn. John, do you have anything you'd like to share with us on God's day?"

"Yes, as a matter of fact, I do." He got up and circled the table so that he was standing behind Julia with his hands on her shoulders. She covered his left hand with her right and they exchanged a glance. "I've asked Julia to marry me and she's done me the honor of saying yes."

Absolute silence settled over the dining room. Belle's eyes widened and she waved both hands in front of her face, pressing her lips together.

Muriel found her voice first. "You what? She what?"

"We're getting married."

"That's...preposterous."

"I'm sorry?" John allowed a tinge of sarcasm to creep into his tone. "Preposterous?"

His mother was flustered but she stuck to her guns. "Yes. Preposterous. You, why, you haven't known each other nearly long enough to consider such a thing. You need to, you need to wait. Until you're ready."

"Really?" John grinned. His grip on Julia's shoulder tightened. "I'd have thought you'd want us safely legal *before* the baby gets here."

Belle's eyes grew impossibly larger and she slapped both hands over her own mouth but squealed anyway."

Muriel glanced her way. "Belle, go to your room."

"But--"

"Your room, Belle. Now. Go to your room, right this minute."

Belle jumped up and ran off. When her footsteps on the stairs had died away Muriel turned her attention to her husband. "Edgar? Dear? Do you want to take your son into the other room and have a word with him?"

If she hadn't made such a point of him being the head of the household, Julia thought, it might not have been quite so obvious that he was not. He nodded once, face shocked and solemn, looked at John and made a motion with his head to indicate the living room. John squeezed Julia's shoulder and gave her a questioning look. She bobbed her head a little and he winked at her and reluctantly followed his father.

"This is completely unacceptable," Muriel said as soon as they were alone. "I don't know what you think you're doing, but you simply cannot marry into my family."

"John disagrees."

"John is foolish and easily manipulated. He will be made to see reason. You must understand. You're not like us. You're..."

"The word you're looking for is Black," Julia prompted.

"I'm not racist," Muriel snapped. "I'm simply pointing out the obvious. The two of you have nothing in common."

"We have a child in common."

"That's not something for an unmarried woman to be proud of." Muriel paced the room, wringing her hands. "Obviously abortion is out of the question, but adoption is a perfectly acceptable option. You'll have to confess to the Father, but the church will help us place the baby in a suitable Christian home."

"We're not going to do anything of the sort," Julia said firmly. "John and I are going to get married and make a home and raise our child."

"No, you're not."

"Yes, we are. We're telling you and your husband as a courtesy, but our relationship isn't a democracy and you don't get a vote. You have absolutely no say in this whatsoever and you might as well get used to the idea."

Muriel froze and stood like a statue, the only movement about her person the trembling of her lower lip. The room smelled of cooking and potpourri and Avon perfume and Julia was conscious of Belle hiding behind the railing at the top of the stairs, peeking down at them.

"I want you to leave my home," Muriel said, voice hard, not looking at Julia.

"Certainly," Julia agreed readily. "I will be happy to leave your home. But just so we're perfectly clear," she stepped close to the other woman, invading her personal space and drawing her eyes up, "I'm taking your son with me."

Later, when she and John were driving away through sunshine that was brighter for the polished darkness they'd left behind, she caught his hand and studied his profile. He looked sad and a sliver of insecurity shivered through her.

"Do you have regrets? About us?" she asked.

He glanced over at her, tightened his fingers around hers.

"I have...unfulfilled wishes," he said.

She tipped her head, letting her expression carry the question and he gave her a sad smile.

"I wish they cared how happy you make me. And I wish that they'd be happy for me too."

———♥———

"And then we went to my folks house and told them," Julia said, leaning her elbow on the corner of Min's desk and propping her chin in her hand. Min was searching her desk drawers, trying to find fresh batteries for the tape player. Her expression was thoughtful and Julia wondered if, although Min couldn't actually hear her, she was aware, on some level, of what she was saying.

"Dad dragged John outside and Mom and I screamed at each other for twenty minutes about freedom and choices and me quitting my masters program to become a white boy's housewife. When we finally reached a detente and went looking for the men, they were sitting out back in lawn chairs drinking beer together and Daddy was telling John about the time he interviewed Cool Papa Bell."

Min slammed the bottom desk drawer and Julia sighed.

"I wish I knew where Daddy is right now. We lost him, you know, when Jude was not quite two. Massive heart attack. He died in his sleep. I wasn't even sure I believed in an afterlife, but I always figured that if there was such a thing, at least my dad would be waiting for me when I got here. But now I'm here and I'm all alone and I don't have any idea where he is or how to reach him."

Chapter Eighteen

Walls Come Tumbling Down

[Style Council, 1985]

"Have you ever googled yourself?"

"That's an awfully personal question," Julia said. "What is that? Is it dirty? It sounds dirty."

Citizens of the twenty-first century spoke such an odd language. They tweeted and Facebooked and snap chatted and instagrammed. The receptionist's teenage daughter had come in to explain that she overslept and missed school because her bff's boo had ghosted her so she lit him up on his wall and her notifications had blown up her phone all night.

It all seemed to make sense to the living but to Julia it was just so much gibberish.

She was sitting on one of the file cabinets in the squad room, as high off the floor as she could get. It was a cool day and she was chilly in just her nightgown so she climbed like a cat. (They'd talked, she and John, about getting Jude a kitten or a puppy. That was one more thing she hadn't lived to do.) The room was perceptibly warmer up there. Min was at her desk, doing paperwork from her last patrol and Oliver had just emerged from Donaldson's office with his odd question.

"Maybe once or twice when I was in high school," Min said, frowning a little. "Why?"

"Donaldson googled himself."

"So it is dirty." Julia pulled her feet up, sitting cross legged and carefully tucking the hem of her sleep shirt around her cold toes.

Oliver seemed equal parts amused and disconcerted.

Min just rolled her eyes.

"Of course he did. He was on Crimewatch the other night. He wanted to see if anyone was talking about him."

"Well, someone is."

"Oh?"

"A cold case blogger called Dr. Justice. He has an offbeat theory about the Lodge murder."

Min tipped her head and raised her eyebrows. Oliver slid his chair over beside her desk and dropped into it. There was no one that he could see in the room but the two of them but he still glanced around before he spoke, leaning in close and lowering his voice.

"He thinks Donaldson killed her."

"What?" Min's surprised reply was louder than she intended and she slapped a hand over her own mouth before repeating the question at a lower volume. "What?"

"Dr. Justice thinks Donaldson killed Julia Lodge."

"Why?"

"I don't know. I just caught the beginning of the freak out. He remembered I was in the room, slammed his computer shut and told me to go find something to do. I know he knew her."

"He didn't just know her," Min said, reaching for her own computer. "He arrested her."

"What? Why am I just now finding this out? How did you know?" He rolled himself around her desk and came up behind her so he could look over her shoulder as her hands moved across the keyboard.

"Donaldson told me. Well, Dr. Dalton sort of made him. He saw her with her white husband and assumed she was a hooker."

"Of course he did." Oliver read from the computer screen. "A small mind in a small town."

"Hey!" Julia's head snapped up. "That was a newspaper headline! That was a newspaper headline more than thirty years ago! Can you read that on your computer? Can you do that? Do you *know* how amazing your technology is?"

"Oh my god," Min said. "It was on her *wedding day*."

"Yeah. Muriel was very smug about that," Julia remembered. "My bitch of a mother-in-law? In some ways that was the worst part of it. She told Belle, 'you can't blame the officer. Girls have to take responsibility for how they present themselves. If you dress like a hooker, people are going to think you're a hooker. Bad things happen to bad girls.'"

"Dalton said Donaldson became the poster boy for racist cops in Oregon," Min remembered.

"Not just Oregon," Oliver said, "from the sound of it." He read from the screen, "for several weeks Donaldson's name was a household word, synonymous with racist. Lawmakers and news analysts debated the prevalence of Donaldsons in police departments across the country and he became the butt of jokes on late-night television. While some defended him on the grounds that he was young and inexperienced, public opinion ran strongly against him."

"I have wondered...." Min trailed off.

"Wondered what?" Oliver prompted.

"The Millers said she brought Jude to their door while the man she was with waited by her car. If she was in trouble, why didn't she ask them for help? She could have just gone inside and had them close the door and call the police."

"The theory has always been that she just wanted her son safe and that she was afraid if she said anything he'd hurt them both."

Min shook her head. "The Millers couldn't describe him. If he was too far away for them to see, he was too far away to intervene."

"She must not have realized she was in danger."

"Which suggests that the man was someone she trusted."

"Like her husband."

"Or a cop. Think about it. It would have been so easy. 'Your husband's been in an accident. You need to come with me. It's bad. Is there someone who can watch your son?'"

"The Millers never mentioned a uniform," Oliver objected. "Surely they'd have noticed if the guy was in a police uniform."

Min shrugged. "He could have said, 'I'm off-duty. I heard the call and volunteered to come get you.' There was no phone at the beach house. She wouldn't have known where her husband was or what he was doing."

"And how, according to your theory, did Donaldson know she was there alone?"

Julia stilled as a memory bubbled to the surface. She was in her car, waiting at a stoplight in Waldport, when she felt eyes on her. Glancing to the side she found Donaldson, in his police cruiser, sitting on the cross street. He got the light and drove slowly through the intersection, turning his head to stare at her as he passed.

Julia shuddered with the remembered sensation of a chill snaking its way up her spine. She'd seen Donaldson as she drove alone through Waldport. But she didn't know when it had happened. It could have been the day before she disappeared. It could have been some random early August day any of the five years before that.

Donaldson's door opened. Min and Oliver flinched guiltily and moved apart. Min's hand brushed across her keyboard.

"What are you doing?" Donaldson's voice was harsh. Accusing.

"MVA last night," Min said. "I'm finishing up the paperwork."

He turned his attention to Oliver.

" I'm just trying to get someone besides me interested in lunch. Seriously. Chinese?"

"I'll take a number 47," Min said. "White rice."

"White? Not fried?"

"Last time I got fried there were eggshells in it."

"Okay then." Oliver looked to Donaldson. "Lieutenant?"

"Hard pass." The senior officer returned to his office, closing the door firmly behind himself.

Oliver leaned close to Min again.

"So are we seriously thinking that *Donaldson* is a suspect?"

"No. Of course not." Nonetheless her voice, to Julia's ear, held a note of uncertainty. She dug a small purse out of a drawer in her desk and handed Oliver a couple of bills to pay for her lunch. He folded them and stood to leave but paused as she spoke again.

"He has her necklace. Did you know? He carries it around in his pocket all the time. Like a talisman, I suppose."

"Right," Oliver said. "A talisman. Or a trophy…"

Chapter Nineteen

Love Is Reason

[A-Ha, 1985]

"The bags marked with a 'W' supposedly represent everything of the Lodges' that was in the beach house here after Julia disappeared."

Donaldson and the two younger deputies had finished with the cassette tapes and were moving on to the rest of the things in the evidence cartons, even as the hour grew late. Julia looked on with interest as they opened box after box to reveal her own, familiar belongings. Each item was packed into its own evidence bag, some tiny and some, like the bag with her comforter, huge.

"I didn't even use that comforter," she said as if they could hear her. "I brought it in case it got cold at night, but it was warm enough I didn't even unpack it."

"At the end of the week, when it was time for the Lodges to leave the beach house, John was supposedly too distracted by her disappearance to worry about their belongings. His sister and the landlady packed the stuff up into the boxes and suitcases Julia had brought it out in. It was mostly still sitting in a corner of John Lodge's garage when I got a search warrant in mid-February. Some of the boxes had been rifled through. They'd needed Jude's clothes and toys and the full-sized bedding was no longer there. It occurred to me that he might have destroyed it but of course I can't prove that. I did check the mattress in the beach house and found some truly disgusting traces of various bodily fluids, but nothing that suggested murder."

"What about the other stuff?" Min asked. She pulled Jude's toy whip out of one of the cartons and turned it in her hand to study it.

"Kinky," Oliver said.

"Just things in the house that caught my eye," Donaldson told her. "Anything that seemed suspicious to me. That, for instance. Lodge insists it was for a Halloween costume for the kid--"

"It *was* for a Halloween costume for Jude," Julia protested.

"--but it seems to me like something you'd use for sex play."

"Yeah, well, not all of us are into Nazi spanking porn."

"How is that relevant, though?" Min asked.

"Just an insight into their relationship," Donaldson said. "Was she a dominatrix? Did he secretly resent that? Was he domineering? A little slave/master fantasizing?"

Julia sat on his desk. "You're a disgusting and despicable human being." She focused on his breast pocket, where her necklace rested. By concentrating she could see it clearly now, like she was looking at it though a cup of strong tea. She reached for it, but he moved at the last second and her fingertips went into his chest. A tingle of energy shivered through her. She could feel the rhythm of his pulse and the sickly sensation of blood. He shuddered and pulled away.

"There has to be a reason he killed her."

"He didn't kill me."

"Did you ever consider that maybe he didn't kill her?" Min asked.

Donaldson gave her a disgusted look. "No. And neither should you."

Julia flicked a pen on his desk and it tumbled to the floor. She could move things out in the open about half the time now, providing no one was actually watching the thing that she wanted to move. Trying to affect something while someone was looking at it was like trying to use a public restroom quickly while someone stood outside the stall door and tapped their foot.

"But it's a possibility," Min insisted. "Don't you think we should keep an open mind until we have proof? Or are you determined to convict him whether he's guilty or not?"

Donaldson jumped up. Julia was reaching for her necklace again and as he moved she caught it and pulled it free but it slipped through her hand and landed on the floor beneath his chair. He never even noticed.

"What the hell do you mean by that?"

The younger deputy backed off but didn't drop it. "It seems sometimes like you're determined to convict John Lodge whether he's actually guilty or not."

"Are you accusing me of trying to frame him for murder?"

"No, I just--"

"Because I might be a lot of things, but a crooked cop isn't one of them. I would *never* want to be a party to convicting an innocent man."

"But--"

"John Lodge is not an innocent man. He left Portland the night his wife was murdered and for thirty years he's refused to tell anyone where he went or what he was doing. That is not the behavior of an innocent man. He killed her, as sure as I'm standing here. And I intend to find out how, and why, and see that he finally faces a judge and jury for it. Because that's my goddamned job."

"But he loved her," Min protested.

"Oh, for God's sake. Think with your badge instead of your vagina."

Min's face went completely white, then flushed. Oliver looked up, shocked, and Donaldson stepped back, pressed his lips together, and turned away.

"I'm going home," he said. "Put all this stuff back before you leave."

He took his windbreaker from its hook by the door and left, closing the door carefully behind himself. Julia's heart lay unnoticed on the floor and she settled into his vacant chair, relieved to not be dragged home with him for a change.

Min was shaking as she dropped into the nearest chair.

"He shouldn't have said that," Oliver said. "That was over the line. If you want to report him, I'll back you up."

She laughed bitterly. "What good would that do? I'd just get a pat on the head and a lecture about how Donaldson is 'old school' and didn't mean anything by it."

"If nothing else, the sheriff would make him apologize."

"A forced apology is meaningless. And Donaldson would just say I've gotten too close to the case. He'd use it as an excuse to have me reassigned. I don't want to be reassigned. I want to see this case to the end."

"Yeah. Okay, I understand. But if you change your mind, I'm here."

"Thank you."

The two started putting Julia's things back in the evidence cartons. They worked in silence several minutes before Oliver broke it with a show of reluctance.

"Listen," he said, "I know you don't want to hear this. But Donaldson might be a bastard. He is a bastard. But he's also a pretty smart cop. And statistically, most murder victims are killed by someone close to them."

She sighed and slapped the lid on the box she'd just filled.

"He loved her. I know. I've talked to him. Listened to him. I was there when he saw her body for the first time. Women know these things. Women can tell. When we get fooled about love, it's because we're fooling ourselves. I'm not fooling myself. John Lodge loved his wife."

"Okay. I'm not disagreeing. If you say he loved her, I'm sure you're right. He loved her. But," Oliver reached over and touched Min's shoulder, his voice gentle, "that doesn't mean he didn't kill her."

Chapter Twenty

I Knew You Were Waiting

[Aretha Franklin and George Michael, 1986]

It had rained early. Now a bright sun was burning off the morning mist, sparkling among the leaves and providing a warm counterpart to a fresh, cool breeze. The trees here were a mix of deciduous and evergreens and Julia stepped carefully across the dark earth, avoiding pine cones. Dappled light played across the shoulders and backs of the law officers moving around her and the morning smelled of coffee and pine with a hint of diesel from the tow truck waiting up on the road.

As the crow flies they were maybe three miles from the cave where Julia's body had washed up, but it was much farther by the road. As Min had predicted, the property was deserted. A house several hundred yards to the west had burned decades before and the land was owned by a member of the family that had lived there. He had moved to California after the fire and never returned. It was accessed by a dirt road. The old driveway was long overgrown, nothing showing now but faint traces of ruts among young trees.

In 1986 it had still been clear enough to admit a vehicle. Just over halfway between the road and the shell of the house an overgrown clearing gave access to the wooded ravine where Julia's car lay hidden under a pile of brush. In the thirty-plus years it had been there soil had collected among the debris and weeds and small bushes grew on top of it. At some point a falling branch had knocked the driver's side mirror loose and it dangled at an awkward angle. It was this mirror that had caught the early light. Otherwise, even searching the pictures with a magnifying glass, it would likely have remained hidden until someone came to do something with the land.

Donaldson raised one hand and called for attention.

"Okay, people. This is what we're going to do. Photographers first. I want pictures of this thing from every angle. Close-ups and wide-shots. You know what to do. When that's done, we're going to need samples of the brush and crap growing on it. This gentleman," he indicated a man in a tan coat, "is Professor Darden from Oregon State University. They're going to analyze the...how do I wanna put this, Doc?"

"The ecosystem, perhaps, that's grown up around this vehicle?" the professor offered. "We're going to examine the materials that were used to cover the car, the plants that have grown on and around them, the materials under the car, and any traces of living creatures we find. Insect colonies, snake sheds, anything like that. The goal is to pinpoint exactly when the car was left here. We'll need samples of everything and we'll need clear records of where those samples came from."

"Everyone understand?" Donaldson asked.

The assorted law officers nodded and he continued.

"After we get pictures and the first round of samples we'll clean off the car and search it here. Then we're going to trailer it back to the state crime lab at Clackamas so they can go over it with a fine-tooth comb. When the car is gone we'll split into two groups. One group will concentrate on the ground under where the car is now sitting. The other will search this entire property for anything that might be connected to our case. Everyone clear on that?" He looked around. "Good. Let's go, people."

While the photographers went to work, Julia hung back, staying close to Min. Darden was standing nearby as well. He was a tall and lean with a deep tan, grey hair, and a pointed salt-and-pepper beard. Sharp hazel eyes followed the proceeding with a quick interest. After a couple of minutes he shed closer to Min and struck up a conversation with the young deputy.

"It's just fascinating to be part of this," he said. "You know, I remember when she disappeared. I actually spoke to, I think it was her sister-in-law. She was organizing search parties. Not this far inland, of course. It never even occurred to anyone to look clear over here, I don't think. I just remember how desperate her family was to find her. Do you think her husband killed her?"

Min shrugged, uncomfortable. "Detective Donaldson does," she hedged.

"Do you?"

She looked around, making sure, Julia thought, that she wouldn't be overheard by the other law officers. "I don't, no."

"Do you have any theories?"

"No, that's the problem. It's one thing to say I don't think he did it, but when I can't offer any viable alternatives, well..."

"No one's willing to listen to what you have to say?"

"Not really."

"Listen, I know he was really young, but has anyone talked to the son? He was right there, right? Maybe he knows something. Even if he doesn't know he knows."

"I've talked to him myself. He remembers bits and pieces of that day, but nothing that helps any so far as I can see. The last memory he has of his mom is her singing him to sleep, and I'm not even sure that memory is reliable, although I wouldn't tell him that."

"Why do you say that?"

"Oh, it just seems a bit fanciful to me. He remembers the beach glowing blue outside the window."

"Does he, now? That's interesting." Darden drew a breath. Julia recognized from experience with her own father that the professor was on the verge of a lecture, but whatever he was going to say was lost as Donaldson dog-whistled at Min.

"Hey! Earth to Min! You gonna help us any time today or you just want to stand around looking homely?"

She rolled her eyes and hurried over to the car. They'd finished with the photography and taken their samples and now the law officers all pitched in to clear away the brush and debris. Julia blinked back a sudden sting of tears as her car emerged.

She hadn't loved the car. She'd bought it herself while she was at school, too proud to ask her parents for help, and it was what she could afford. It was a weird shade of gray that turned green under stormlight, the back seat was ripped and stained from before she got it and there was a strange rattle that their mechanic couldn't find.

But it was hers. She'd spent hundreds of hours behind that wheel. She'd carried her son in the back seat. Brought home groceries and wedding supplies and Christmas gifts. She'd made love to John there and used it to move out of the dorm and into their house.

Now it sat, forlorn and long-empty, in a hole in the ground. A cop she didn't know levered a heavy branch off the hood and the windshield below was spider webbed with cracks. The tires were rotting into the soil and rust speckled the body.

She leaned against the grime-encrusted windows and tried to see inside. Jude's booster seat was still strapped into place. The empty plastic travel mug she'd drunk coffee from on her way to Waldport sat in the cup holder between the front seats. The passenger seat was still strewn with cassette tapes she'd listened to on the trip and not replaced in their holder in the passenger-side foot well. She saw Paul Simon's Graceland album, A-Ha, Dire Straits, and Cyndi Lauper.

While it was down in the ravine the doors wouldn't open. Donaldson used a lock pick to open the trunk and Julia looked in to find it still contained everything she and John had loaded for her trip that she hadn't unloaded when she arrived at the beach house. There were grocery sacks filled with the majority of their canned goods, two cases of soda pop, a case of beer, the spare tire and a roadside emergency kit with flares and a jumper cable.

"Looks like supplies for their vacation," Donaldson observed. "Did she leave it in here or did someone pack it back up again?"

"I left it there," Julia said, frustrated that he couldn't hear her. "I figured I'd let John lug it in."

Donaldson shrugged and slammed the trunk. "We'll

leave it for the lab to look over. Probably better to wait and open the doors back in the lab as well. Okay, people. Let's get this car out of here."

The law officers moved out of the way and the guys with the tow truck backed into position and went to work affixing chains and preparing to winch the vehicle up onto the trailer. Julia found herself standing once more beside Min. Darden came over, seeking out the young deputy.

"There was something I wanted to ask you about," he said.

"Yes, sir?"

"The boy...you said he told you the beach was glowing blue?"

"That's what he said. I figured he imagined it."

"Not necessarily."

"You mean that can happen?"

"Under the right circumstances, yes. Do you happen to know the phase of the moon that night? I can look it up, if you'll remind me what the date was."

"No, I know it. It was the first night after the new moon."

"So still dark. Yes, that's possible."

"What is?"

Darden shifted. He had a nervous energy about him that he expressed by talking with his hands. "There are dinoflagel-lates--microorganisms--in the sand that emit bioluminescence. Like fireflies. You've heard of fireflies?"

"I've heard of them, yes. I've never seen one."

"We don't have them here but they're common back east, where I grew up. With fireflies, or lightning bugs as they're also called, the tail lights up. They're like blinking Christmas lights. They can be quite bright. Dinoflagellates are much smaller. They just give off a faint blue glow, but if the night is dark enough you can see it sometimes."

"So Jude could have really been remembering."

"He could, yes, but..."

"But?"

"The thing is, dinoflagellates don't usually glow on their own. They have to be disturbed. You see them in the wake of boats travelling at night, or sparking in your footprints when you walk across the sand. If that little boy was seeing them glowing, there had to be something out there disturbing them. Now I suppose it could have been a dog or a raccoon or something."

"But it could have also been a person," Min said. "Someone stalking them on the beach that night."

Chapter Twenty-One

The Sun Always Shines On TV

[A-Ha, 1985]

"You wanted to see me?" Donaldson stuck his head in the door and the young sheriff looked up and beckoned him inside.

"Yeah. Come in. Close the door and have a seat."

Donaldson complied, his forehead wrinkling in consternation. Julia, who had slipped in behind him, took a seat on the windowsill where the sun shone in. She couldn't feel the warmth the way she had in life but she was aware of the energy seeping into her.

She flicked her finger at a red pencil that lay on the bookcase next to her but nothing happened.

"Is something wrong?" Donaldson asked.

The sheriff steepled his fingers and looked at Donaldson over them. "You tell me. I heard a rumor that there was an... incident the other night. Involving Deputy Min?"

Donaldson's mouth tightened and his eyes grew hard. "Did she file a complaint?"

"No. No, she hasn't said a word. I just, you know, I heard it through the grapevine." He actually sang the words.

"I'll bet I know just which grape it was, too."

"You want to tell me what happened?"

The muscles in Donaldson's jaw bunched and he looked to his left. Julia braced herself for bullshit. It was one of his tells, she'd discovered. When he looked to the left before speaking he was preparing to deliver a load of bullshit.

"I lost my temper and said something I shouldn't have,"

he admitted honestly enough.

"So I hear."

Donaldson put his elbows on the sheriff's desk and leaned forward, radiating a sincerity that Julia didn't trust. "Listen. Min is a good cop. She's got a lot of promise. She's intelligent and observant and she has an analytical mind."

"But?"

"*But* she has a hard time separating her heart from her head."

"For example?"

"She wants to believe that John Lodge is innocent."

"That he is or that he might be?"

"I don't see the distinction," Donaldson said, sitting back.

"No? Because it's a pretty important one, I think. It seems to me that Min isn't the only one with an emotional stake in this case."

Up to this point Julia had dismissed the young sheriff as a baby politician, focused on his own ambitions and poorly suited to the position he held. And perhaps to some extent he was, but in that moment her respect for him climbed a notch.

"What do you mean by that?" Donaldson asked, his voice carefully level.

"You want Lodge to be guilty."

"He is guilty!" Donaldson bit off an impatient sigh. "I *believe* he's guilty. Eighty percent of homicide victims knew their killer. Fifty-five percent of adult female victims were murdered by an intimate partner. John Lodge was MIA the night his *wife* was *murdered* and for thirty years he's refused to say where he was or what he was doing."

"So he had opportunity," the sheriff said. "What about means? What about motive?"

"I don't know what his motive was. Yet."

"Means?"

"Maybe."

Julia tensed and leaned forward. He'd been to Clackamas without her, leaving her pendant in his desk for a change, and come back with an air of suppressed excitement.

"There was a toolkit in the trunk of Julia's car when we found it. It included a tire repair kit that came with a pair of tools called a rasp and a needle." He held up one finger, then reached into his inside pocket and came out with a small tool. It consisted of a red plastic handle set at right angles to a short, pointed shaft. When he closed his fist around the handle the shaft protruded from between his first two fingers. "This is the rasp out of the kit in my own trunk. The needle is just like this but the point isn't threaded and it has an eye like the opening in a sewing machine needle. The ME says either could have delivered the fatal blow." He illustrated with a punching motion.

"Did you test them for blood residue? Would there still be traces after all this time?"

"There might be. And we tested the needle. It came back clean. But we couldn't test the rasp because it's missing. To all appearances the kit has never been used. Everything is there and in its place except for the rasp. Lodge claims he has no idea where it went."

"So where do we stand on the investigation?" the sheriff asked.

"I think we have almost enough to charge him. We have possible means and we have opportunity. We don't have motive but his silence and his sister's suicide will work against him with a jury. And Charlie Miller is in hospice care at his home. It's unlikely he'll live long enough for the case to go to trial."

"The DA will still have to tell his lawyer that Charlie said he wasn't the man with her that night. He'll be required to turn it over as exculpatory evidence."

Donaldson bit back an impatient sigh. "Yes, but hearing that he said it won't make as much of an impression as actually hearing him say it would. We'll make sure they understand that he was ill and impaired. And we can put Harriet on the stand to testify that she believes it was him."

"You want to pick him up then?"

Donaldson hesitated while Julia held what passed for her breath.

"I'd like to try one last time to get him to come clean

about the night of the murder. We can hold him for 72 hours before we have to charge him. If he doesn't talk now, with an indictment hanging over his head, he's never going to. But—"

"But?"

"I've learned that Jude is going out of state tomorrow. He's attending a convention in DC. That would be an ideal time to pick up his father. Catch him without that emotional support. I need to go out of town myself this weekend, however."

"Oh?"

Donaldson raised his chin with a sort of defiant pride. "My son is a professional hockey player in the Colorado organization. The team has announced that he's making his NHL debut in Denver Saturday. I want to be there."

"Yes. Of course you do."

Donaldson leaned in again. "How about this? Min wants a chance to clear him. Have her pick him up Saturday morning. She and Oliver have two days to work on him. If he hasn't come clean by Monday morning, I'll take over. If he doesn't talk by the end of the 72 hours, we charge him."

"You run this by the DA?"

"I did. He's tentatively onboard, pending another round of questioning."

"Okay. Let's do it then."

Donaldson nodded, got up and headed for the door. The sheriff stopped him with his hand on the knob. "And Donaldson?"

"Yes?"

"That incident with Min? That needs to not happen again."

———♥———

Before he left Waldport Saturday morning, Donaldson called Min and confirmed that she'd taken John into custody. Julia's heart was there with her husband in the interrogation room but her necklace was in Donaldson's pocket so her spirit traveled with him to Denver.

She didn't know what he was hoping for from the trip. Perhaps he didn't know himself. Whatever it was, he didn't get it.

No one had bothered to tell him that his son was making his NHL debut. He'd learned of it while reading the sports page in the newspaper. Neither his ex-wife nor the boy would answer his calls and he wasn't among the friends and family invited to the game.

The rental car Donaldson picked up at the Denver airport was a midsize Chevy in a nondescript tan color. It came with a map, a Denver area guidebook, and a remote control that had a dead battery. This was something he didn't discover until he tried to lock it at the hotel.

He'd booked a reservation with a national hotel chain but in his haste he'd gotten the wrong location and was across town from the hockey arena. The staff had been kind and sympathetic but the hotel he wanted had no vacancies and there was nothing they could do.

The team was having a banner year. Julia, who knew little about hockey, gathered that they were a generally good team with a loyal fan base. This made tickets hard to come by and Donaldson wound up sitting near the top of the stands with his son and the other players tiny, indistinguishable action figures in the distance.

Rex had been right about the ghosts and Julia watched with interest as they thronged around her, nearly as numerous as their living counterparts. They mingled with the crowd, sat in the boxes with the players, and ran and skated beside them on the ice. None of them paid any attention to her and she didn't try to interact with them.

They announced Donaldson's son and the crowd roared. He stood and cheered with them, smacked the man to his left on the arm and crowed, "that's my boy!"

The stranger beamed back. "I feel the same way," he shouted over the noise. "I've been following that kid since he first got drafted!"

"No," Donaldson tried. "You don't understand." But the stranger had turned away and the moment was lost.

During the intermission between the first and second periods they showed a video clip on the big television above the rink.

"It's always an exciting time here at the Pepsi Center, but tonight we have some extra excitement. We're welcoming a new member of the Avalanche family: Twenty-one year old left wing, Kyle Cavendish. We had a chance, before the game today, to visit with Kyle."

The picture switched to a unidentified room. The young man from the church in Portland was front and center, wearing a Colorado Avalanche sweatshirt, talking to the announcer while two or three dozen people milled around in the background, laughing and eating.

"Kyle," the announcer said, "It's great to be joining you here, surrounded by your friends and your family. So tell me something. Are you excited?"

"Oh, yeah. I am. So excited. I can't even begin to tell you."

"Are you nervous?"

"No. Not really. I mean, a little I guess. But I've just...I've been waiting for this day and dreaming about this day so long that, now that it's here, it just doesn't seem really real. Maybe it will when I skate out on that ice. But all I can say is, I know how hard I've worked, and that I *have* put in the work, and I believe I'm ready. I guess we'll all see when I get out there. Right now it's just so amazing and I'm just trying to soak it all in and, y'know, really appreciate this chance that I've been given. And I'm just going to go out there and do the best I can to help this team and try to do whatever I need to do to win some games for these great fans here."

"Okay, well, we're going to let you get back to your friends in just a second, but first is there anything you'd like to say to those fans?"

"Yeah. Um, yeah. Yes, there is. I know there are a lot of young fans out there and probably a lot of you love this sport the way I do and you're hoping to be here yourself someday. And all I can say is to listen to your trainers and your coaches, but most of all listen to your parents. Because they're the ones who are going to be there for you. My mom, man, my mom hasn't always had it easy but she's stood by me like nobody's business. And I've been so lucky to have a dad I can look up to and turn to. He's not only taught me how to be a good athlete, he's shown me how to be a good man and I only hope I make him proud of me."

Julia blinked in confusion, then whispered, "oh," as a strange man came up beside Kyle and put his arm around the young man's shoulders.

"Is this your dad?" the announcer asked.

"Yeah. This is him, man. This is my dad."

"He's not your son." In the packed, noisy arena, probably only Julia heard Donaldson's whisper. "He's my son."

The man squeezed Kyle in a huge hug. "This is my kid," he announced. "This is my boy. I love this kid so much and I am so proud of him right now!"

The video ended. Donaldson ordered another beer and watched the rest of the game in silence.

When it was over and Colorado had won, they left. The parking lot, according to another lost soul, held over four thousand cars. With his remote control not working it took Donaldson over an hour to find where he'd parked.

The area around the arena was still busy but once they left it behind they found the city asleep. The odd bar or fast food place were puddles of light and activity. Towering business buildings had darkened all but security lights. The road they were on was four lanes wide and completely deserted except for them.

At regular intervals they passed through cones of yellow illumination from the streetlights. Donaldson drove in silence but his cheeks glistened.

Julia sat in the passenger seat and wondered if she were a horrible person because she couldn't muster any sympathy for him. He'd built this future brick by brick every time he'd put himself before his family.

Everything he'd thrown away, she'd had stolen.

The tires whined along the pavement. They passed empty shopping centers and a deserted mall, closed restaurants, dark boutiques, silent grocery stores. Barren parking lots stretched out in every direction; block upon lonely block of unoccupied asphalt.

Julia stared out the window and watched it go by. She wondered what her little boy had grown up to be. What his wife's name was and what her granddaughters looked like.

Chapter Twenty-Two

The Man's Too Strong

[Dire Straits, 1985]

John sat in the interrogation room, hands folded on the table top and an untouched glass of water sitting beside him. Julia hugged the two-way mirror, hand pressed against the unforgiving glass. She longed to go to his side, but didn't dare leave the observation room. The cops were being careful with what doors they opened when and she was afraid she'd get shut out altogether, unable to even see or hear what was happening.

Donaldson was determined to "break him," but to Julia's eyes he looked long-broken. Shattered years before and never properly put back together. His blond hair had gone white, his blue eyes faded. Ragged stubble covered his cheeks. Broad shoulders slumped, rounded and worn-down. His clothes were too big, old and worn. John had never been a large man, but he'd been imposing. A big personality, generous of spirit, with a huge heart that encompassed everyone in his orbit.

Now he was a tired old man, as much a ghost in his own way as Julia was.

Oliver cracked open the door to the observation room just enough to stick his head in.

"Jude's here."

Donaldson nodded tersely. He was focused, like a bird dog that had scented a flight of geese. "Send him in."

There was a brief moment of anticipation, time for Julia to take the illusion of a breath, and the door to the other room opened to admit her son. Jude was dressed more casually this time in jeans and a polo shirt with a handful of gold chains tangled about his neck. He took the chair across from his father.

John looked up at him. "I'm sorry," he said simply.

"Dad--no." Jude reached out to him.

When Jude was small, in Julia's memory such a short time ago, both his little hands had fit between hers. When he'd play outside in the winter and come in chilled, she'd strip off his sodden mittens and cradle his fists between her palms, rubbing them and blowing on them to get them warm. Now they dwarfed his father's.

He leaned down, making eye contact. "They're not going to let this go this time, Dad. They think they have enough circumstantial evidence to charge you with murder. You've got to tell them what happened that night."

John barely moved, a slight lift of one shoulder, a slight shake of the head. "I can't," he said helplessly.

"Dad..." Jude shook his own head. He scooted his chair closer to the table and the squeal of the chair legs against the tile floor echoed in the little room. "Listen to me. I don't know what your secret is, or why you've kept it all these years, but there's something you need to understand.

"I know you. I know you better than anyone. You're the one who raised me. You took care of me every time I was sick. You held me every time I was sad. And I remember *everything*. I remember you working two jobs so I could play sports and take music lessons. I remember you letting me spend holidays with Mom's family, even though you weren't welcome and it meant you'd spend the day alone. I remember you chasing away the monsters when I woke up from a nightmare, and coming to my school plays and my baseball games and making sure I had everything I needed, even if it meant that you went without.

"Now that I'm a father myself, I only hope I can be half the dad to my girls that you were to me. No, hush," he said, when John would have interrupted. "*Listen* to me. I love you. And there is nothing--*nothing*--you could say to me right now that would ever change that one iota."

John looked his son in the eye.

"Even if I tell you I murdered your mother?"

In the observation room Donaldson, standing next to Julia, tensed. His knuckles whitened around the ink pen he carried in his left hand and he leaned in toward the window.

Jude met his father's gaze.

"Even that."

John put his hands flat on the table, not looking away. "I *didn't*."

Jude mirrored his father's pose. "I *know*," he said.

"Oh, for fuck's sake," Donaldson growled, pacing away. "Well, then--"

"It's not about me, Dad," Jude said, before he could finish the sentence.

"It's always about you," John countered. "You've been the most important thing in my life for a very long time now. If you believe me, that's all that matters to me."

"But it isn't all that matters to me. I need for you to be okay. I need for you to be there for my girls, and not just in prison visits. And I *need* to know what happened to my mother. And that asshole in there isn't going to look for the real killer until you tell him what you know."

John turned his palms up in a helpless gesture. "I made a promise," he said.

"Anyone you love enough to protect this long, loves you back enough to not want you to suffer," Jude countered. "They will release you."

"They can't. They never can."

"Tell me this, then. I'm your son. Who else is there, in all the world, that you owe your allegiance more than me?"

John couldn't hold his gaze then, but looked down. Tears, like the first raindrops, struck the table beneath his bent head. Julia, flat against the two-way mirror, trying to claw her way through the glass, knew the exact second when he capitulated.

"The roses," he said, scrubbing one hand down the side of his face, "the wine and the roses were for your mother. I always loved her. I only loved her."

"What happened, Pop?"

"I knew all along there was a chance I'd get done early, but you could never count on anything, working for that bastard. I figured it would be better to surprise you and your mom than to disappoint you, so I didn't say anything."

Jude reached to the side to pick up the glass of water and set it in front of his father. John paused to take a sip.

"I worked late that day, finished the rest of my work so I wouldn't have to go in on Friday. I stopped and bought the wine and the flowers and went home to change clothes before I headed out. I was just on the point of leaving, I had my hand on the doorknob to go, when the phone rang."

He stopped talking again.

"Dad?" Jude prompted. "Who was on the phone? Dad?"

"Belle," John said finally. "It was your Aunt Belle. Crying so hard I could hardly understand her. She was stranded at a gas station in the middle of nowhere and she needed me." He raised his head, meeting Jude's eyes, but his gaze was distant. He was seeing things that had happened years ago and Julia knew how that felt. "She needed me to come take care of her, because she'd been raped."

Chapter Twenty-Three

Don't Let The Sun Go Down On Me

[George Michael and Elton John, Live Aid Concert, 1985]

"Bullshit," Donaldson said. "This is all bullshit. But it's *good* bullshit."

Oliver frowned. "Sir?"

"Lodge's alibi. Don't tell me you believe it."

"You don't?"

"Hell no. More than three decades and this is the best story he could come up with? It's good though. This is really good."

They were still in the observation room. John and Jude were still on the other side of the glass. Jude had moved to sit on the same side of the table as his father and put an arm around his shoulders. Donaldson paced, watching them and chewing on his pen.

"He's finally given me an alibi. You know what that means?"

Oliver nodded reluctantly. "If you can disprove his alibi it will strengthen the case against him. Did you ever consider he might be telling the truth though?"

"No."

"Min thinks he is."

"I know." Donaldson snorted derisively. "She thinks with her--" he caught something sharp in Oliver's eye and hesitated for a fraction of a second. "Her heart," he said. "That's why I'm sending her in to take his statement. She'll draw him out, because she believes him. The more details the better. The easier it will be to prove he's lying. First I break the alibi, then I break him."

The door to the interrogation room opened and Min entered carrying a notebook and three more bottles of water. She set a bottle down in front of each of the men and took a seat across the table from them.

John sat with his hands flat on the table before him. Min reached out and placed her own smaller hand on one of his. "I realize this is difficult for you," she said, "but I'm going to need to take a statement."

"Does this have to come out?" John asked. "That was the thing she was most afraid of. She was so ashamed. She didn't want anybody to know."

"She didn't do anything wrong."

"I know that. She didn't know that."

"I'll do what I can," she said. "Let's start from the beginning. What time did you leave work?"

"A quarter after six," John said. "I stopped at the grocery store on the way home and bought a dozen roses and a bottle of wine. I paid with my credit card. The phone rang at 7:13. You know all this. You've talked to my coworkers and pulled my credit card and phone records. You've known this for years."

"I know. I know. I just need to get it down on record, as part of your formal statement. You got the call from Belle. What did you do then?"

"I went to her," he said, lifting his shoulders in a quick, irritated shrug. "I went to her as fast as I could. She didn't know where she was, just the name of the highway. The gas station didn't have a sign where she could see it and I drove up and down the road until I found her."

"She was still at the station?"

"She was still in the phone booth, sitting on the ground with her arms wrapped around her knees and her head down. She'd cried herself out and she was just sitting there shaking. No one tried to help her. People passing by just stared at her and gave her a wide berth. She was covered with bruises, but none that showed. And she was--" he broke off and looked to Jude. Jude rubbed his shoulder and nodded encouragement.

"--she was bleeding. Her clothes were bloody. She'd been a virgin and he wasn't gentle."

"What did you do?"

"I had a blanket in the back of the car. I wrapped her in it and drove to the hospital in Corvallis, but she wouldn't get out of the car and she got hysterical when I tried to carry her. She was afraid someone she knew would see her. I tried to reason with her but I couldn't calm her down. I finally had to take her all the way to Salem before she'd agree to go to a hospital."

"What time did you arrive at the hospital?"

"God, I don't know. It was late."

"Your best guess."

"Ten or ten-thirty maybe?"

"And you took her to the emergency room?"

"Yes. They took her right in. There was a woman doctor, thank God, and the nurses were kind. And I called the police but the cop who came was an ass. He asked her what she was wearing and if she were drunk. How many sex partners had she had and what did she do to make the guy think that she was interested in him. And then he told me he couldn't even do anything. It didn't happen in his jurisdiction. We'd have to report it in the county where it happened and there was no way in hell Belle was agreeing to that. That's when she asked me not to tell anyone what happened. I told her I'd have to tell Julia. I couldn't keep a secret like that from my wife. And Julia loved her. And she was wise. She'd have known what to do. Better than I did."

John was staring at the table top. Min paused in her writing and leaned down to catch his eye. "Everything I've heard about your sister tells me she was a lovely young woman. I'm so sorry this happened to her."

He nodded briefly. His face tightened in pain. His eyes were red and tears ran down his cheeks again. He didn't bother to brush them away.

"How did you settle the hospital bill?"

"I paid cash. I had withdrawn money for our vacation earlier in the day."

"What time did you leave the hospital and where did you

go?"

"It was well after midnight. Two-thirty? Three a.m. maybe? I took her home with me to Portland. I wanted to go get Julia but by that time it was so late and I knew she'd be asleep. And Belle was wrung out and needed to rest. The doctor had given her a sleeping pill but she was still afraid that the rapist would show up. So I sat up and guarded her while she slept."

"You left the next morning," Min said. "Did you leave her alone?"

"No, I brought her with me. When I came to Waldport the next morning, Belle was asleep on the back seat of the car. She loved the seashore. I thought we could maybe take care of her at the seashore and somehow eventually she'd be all right. But Julia was gone when I got there and nothing was ever all right again."

"Do you think the rape had something to do with the reason Belle killed herself?"

John laughed bitterly. "Something to do with it? It had *everything* to do with it. I failed my sister. You know that, right?"

"Dad--"

"No, I did. When Julia disappeared the world fell apart. It was like a kind of madness, and all I could think about was finding her. Belle took care of me when I should have been taking care of her. She babysat you and put up flyers and made phone calls and helped organize search parties. And I tried to always be gentle with her, and I'd ask her sometimes if she was okay and she'd always give me a brittle smile and say that she was. And we never spoke of that night again.

"When she got engaged to Wayne Devore I knew she didn't want to marry him. He was just some guy our parents introduced her to. A church deacon from a well-to-do family. Everything they always wanted in a son-in-law. I thought she felt guilty about what happened, and had decided she was being punished for trying to follow her dreams. So I tried to talk her out of it, but I didn't begin to understand how bad it was."

"I'm sorry, but," Min interrupted him, "she thought being raped was some kind of *punishment*?"

"You didn't know our parents," John said. "You know you're not supposed to hide your light under a basket? It says that. Right there in the Bible. But Belle was the brightest light in our family and our folks had been piling baskets on her since the day she was born. She had the most brilliant mind. She could grasp concepts and see connections, understand things in an instant that other people had to study for days. She loved whales and she told me once she thought God loved whales too, so he made it her calling to help save them from humanity."

"Your folks didn't approve?"

"She wanted to go to school and become an oceanographer. They wanted her to marry a successful Catholic boy and settle down to keep house and have babies. She tried so hard to be a good daughter while still following her own path and they criticized and harped on her constantly. When she succeeded she was met with stony silence, but the least little setback was 'God's will asserting itself'. I can still hear my mother's voice."

Julia mouthed the words along with him. "'Bad things happen to bad girls.'"

He stopped to take a drink of water, then held the bottle up and gazed into its depths.

"If they'd known she'd been raped, they *would* have blamed her."

"They must have been pleased when she gave up school and got engaged."

"Oh, they were ecstatic. My strong, independent, Black wife had run off and sweet little Belle had come to her senses. Of course, I knew Julia hadn't just left. She wouldn't do that. To me, maybe, but never to Jude."

"Not to you either, you idiot," Julia whispered, leaning her forehead against the glass.

"And I knew that Belle getting married was bad. I just didn't know how bad. I didn't know that until it was too late."

"Until after she killed herself?"

"Until after she killed herself, when they gave me the note she left. It was addressed to me."

Min glanced through her file. "We were told the note said that Wayne Devore was her true love."

"That was how everyone interpreted it. That wasn't what it said. It said, 'it was Wayne. He was the one.' I still don't know how the situation came about, but my sister killed herself to keep from being forced to marry the man who raped her."

"That's why you took a swing at him at the funeral."

"Yeah. I wanted to do so much more. But Donaldson had already made up his mind that I'd murdered my wife and Rose Meyers was talking about trying to get custody of Jude. I was afraid that if they could make a case that I was violent I'd lose him, and he was the only thing I had left to live for. And it was too late to help Belle anyway. So I did the only thing I still could for her. I kept her secret."

Chapter Twenty-Four

Live To Tell

[Madonna, 1986]

"I'll contact Salem PD," Oliver said, already lifting his phone to his ear. "I doubt there are still medical records, but I'll reach out to the hospital there as well, just in case."

"If they do have records," Donaldson said, "if they ever did--which I doubt--you'll need a search warrant to get your hands on them. Be prepared, just in case." He turned to Min, just back from escorting John and Jude to the front exit. "Wayne Devore. Find him."

"Got it," she said at once, heading for her own desk and opening her computer.

"What are you doing?" Oliver asked. Donaldson glared at him and he held both hands up defensively. "I'm just curious. I've never worked a homicide before. I'm trying to learn here."

"I want to review my original notes from the morning she disappeared, when John came in and tried to file a missing persons report the first time. And I'm going to see if there's an autopsy report on Belle Lodge."

"I've got Wayne Devore," Min said. The two men turned to look at her.

"Already?" Oliver asked.

"He was a student at OSU, like Belle. I found him in the alumni directory. I don't have a home address yet, but I will in a minute. He's in Portland, working for a nonprofit affiliated with the Catholic Church. Hope House. They run a shelter for the children of women who are incarcerated. Devore is the assistant director of an outreach program they do that provides mentoring and development opportunities for underprivileged children and teens."

"Sounds like a salubrious fellow," Donaldson said. "Get me an address where I can find him. I want very much to hear his side of this story."

——❤——

The words "HOPE HOUSE" were painted in ornate blue script on a white wooden sign, sharing space with a cross and a pair of stylized doves. The sign hung on an old, red brick building, partially covering the remains of an older sign, flaking off the bricks themselves, that had once read "Bartlett and Barrows Bottling Co."

A small parking lot to the side of the building still served its original purpose. The larger lot to the back had been fenced in. The asphalt had been ripped up to make way for flower and vegetable gardens. They ringed in a yard that contained a basketball court with poles midway to string tennis or volleyball nets. There was a barbecue pit beside the stairs leading to the building and the old loading dock now held groups of picnic tables.

The low clouds had stalled against the mountains to the east. Late afternoon sun, slipping below the west edge of the storm front, lit their underside an eerie blue-black and cast a preternatural golden glow across downtown Portland. Julia followed Donaldson through a red metal door into the building.

The thick, warped glass in the old windows twisted the odd light into a semblance of a rainbow. Julia thought of Belle and grief and fury vibrated through her with the energy of the sun.

Unlike the detective, she didn't doubt John's story for an instant.

The door let them into a narrow hallway presided over by an unattended desk. Voices came from behind closed doors on the right. Double metal doors to the left were propped open to a gymnasium, busy with bouncing balls and whistles. Julia poked her head in and noted about a dozen schoolgirls in white tee shirts and red shorts running basketball drills on an indoor court.

Donaldson knocked his knuckles on the desk and shouted. "Hello? Anybody here? Hey! Hello?"

A young redhead wearing blue jeans and a red tee shirt came out of one of the closed rooms to the right. Over her left breast was a bright-colored paper patch that read "hi! My name is SISTER MARIAN."

"Oh, I'm sorry! I wasn't expecting anyone to come in. Can I help you?"

Donaldson ogled her in his customary offensive manner. "You're a nun?"

"Um...yes. What can I do for you?"

"Aren't you supposed to be wearing a habit and fishnet stockings?"

She frowned at him. "No."

He sighed. "You're destroying all my fantasies." He pulled out his badge. "I'm looking for Wayne Devore. I understand he works here?"

"Oh, yes. Deacon Devore has an office upstairs. Shall I call up and announce you?"

"Just tell me where to find him."

Sister Marian directed him around a corner and up a flight of stairs. "The deacon's office is the last door on the right."

Julia followed Donaldson. As they climbed the flight of stairs and traversed the hallway, she noticed electrical outlets at regular intervals. She could *see* the electrons buzzing with potential inside the slots and when she reached out her hands in passing thin wisps of energy streamed towards her. She drew them in and hoarded the power and wondered if she could reach into Devore's body and draw his beating heart out of his chest.

She wondered if the light would still come for her, and, if it did, where it would take her.

The doors on the second floor were mostly plain slabs of dark wood, but Devore's was more ornate, with brass hardware and a marbled light, his name and title stenciled on the glass. Donaldson pulled it open and went in without knocking.

Julia edged in before he could close it firmly behind him

and got her first look at Wayne Devore.

He looked like a banker or an insurance agent. A gray-haired man in late middle age, he was neither short nor tall. In youth he had probably been considered athletic but now he tended toward belly fat. He was conservatively dressed in a dark suit made of expensive material. His eyes, behind thick glasses, were almost colorless.

His hands were soft, his fingers thick and pale with perfectly-manicured nails. Julia thought of him touching Belle with them and wanted to hurt him. She moved restlessly around the room, so furious she frightened herself, and the ceiling light flickered when she passed the switch.

Devore was sitting behind his desk, studying something on a laptop computer. He closed it and stood when Donaldson came in.

"Can I help you with something?" he asked suspiciously.

"Wayne Devore?"

"Yes."

"Detective Manfred Donaldson." He flashed his badge again. "I'm investigating the murder of Julia Lodge."

"Oh, yes. My poor fiancée's sister-in-law. Are you sure she was murdered? Belle's parents thought she ran away."

"She was murdered. Her remains were found last summer? You didn't know?"

"I'm not in touch with anyone in that family anymore," he said. "Belle's parents are dead, you know, and her brother and I have never seen eye to eye."

Donaldson chose a chair in front of the desk and dropped into it. "Tell me about her brother," he said.

"John?" Devore shifted uncomfortably. "I didn't actually know him that well," he hedged. "I didn't meet him until some time after his wife went missing. Not until after Belle and I were engaged, in fact."

"How did you and Belle get together?"

"We met through our families. My grandparents attended church with her parents. They introduced us. John and his family were living in Portland when Belle and I began our courtship. He objected to our marriage, for some reason. I suspect he was so unhappy in his own marriage he couldn't bear the thought of us being happy."

Donaldson leaned forward. "I always wondered if John didn't have some...*unnatural* attachment to his sister, if you know what I mean."

Devore sat back, his eyes narrowed and his head tipped to his left. "You may be right," he said. "I've never entirely accepted that Belle really chose to take her own life. I thought she was simply nervous about her wedding day and accidentally overdosed. But if she did intend to kill herself, that may have had something to do with it. You know she left a note for him. She wanted him to know that I was her true love. I've always wondered about that."

Devore had Belle's picture, framed and matted in black, sitting next to a radio on a shelf in the corner. It was an old picture, even to Julia. For some reason he had chosen to remember his lost bride as a 12-year-old girl in a Catholic school uniform. Julia rested her fist beside the photo and the radio spontaneously crackled to life. Madonna's Like A Virgin blasted out.

Devore jumped, got up and turned it off. The ceiling light flickered again and he eyed it nervously.

"This old building needs new wiring," he said. "I don't know where we'll find the money."

Donaldson waited for him to sit back down.

"John claims that he spent the night his wife disappeared taking care of Belle." He paused a beat, watching Devore. "He claims you raped her."

Devore stiffened. "What a reprehensible thing to say! Imagine sullying his sister's memory by suggesting such a thing."

Julia hovered behind his chair, purposely drawing the heat from his body. The energy swirled around her like static electricity. She could feel her hair floating around her head. "Tell the truth," she whispered in his ear. "Tell the truth. Tell the truth. Tell the man the goddamn truth."

"Listen," Donaldson said, "John Lodge killed his wife. I know that. I know it with every fiber of my being and I *have* known it for over thirty years. But I could never convict him because without a body I couldn't prove she was dead. And I couldn't break his alibi as long as he refused to give me one. But now I have a body and he's given me an alibi. If I can prove that he was lying about where he was that night, I can finally put that bastard away.

"I know it was a hell of a long time ago, but is there any way you can figure out where you were and what you were doing? And is there any way you would be able to prove it? Pictures, class schedules, phone records? Anything?"

"Well, yes," Devore said. "Yes, absolutely. It just so happens that I went to a convention in San Francisco that weekend."

Donaldson sat back. "Really?"

"He's lying," Julia said. "Look at him. He's *lying*!"

"Well, yes. I left Corvallis Thursday morning. I rode with one of my frat brothers, Earl Stanton. I'll give you his phone number. He'll tell you I was with him the whole day. I have pictures, actually. From that weekend. It was a Christian leadership conference. Here."

He opened a lower drawer, rifled through the hanging files there, and came up with a sheaf of brittle, yellowed papers and faded photographs. "Here's the itinerary and a copy of my hotel bill, too. Will that help?"

Donaldson took the bundle and leafed through it. "Yes, it will," he said. "This should help a lot. Thank you."

He rose and turned for the door. Julia stared at him in disbelief.

"What the hell, Donaldson? You're just going to take his word for it? Just like that?"

Donaldson paused, his left hand full of papers and his right resting on the polished brass doorknob. He was looking down and, when he spoke, his voice was almost sad.

"You know," he said, "it's a funny thing. I actually met the victim, did you know that? The first week I was on the job. I was the one who took the missing person report when she disappeared and I was the one who did the legwork then. I followed up on it when she was still missing six months later.

I was the only one who believed something really happened to her--she didn't just leave. I'm the one who worked it as a cold case for thirty years and when her remains finally came to light, I'm the one who took charge of the investigation."

"Really?" Devore asked from behind him.

"Yeah. Really. In a lot of ways, this case has defined my career. My life even. And I don't know where I was the night that Julia Lodge disappeared. " He turned around ever so slowly, raised his head and looked Wayne Devore in the eye. The other man paled and shrank away. "So how is it you have an alibi prepared?"

Chapter Twenty-Five

Under Pressure

[David Bowie and Queen, 1982]

Devore sat in the interrogation room, in the same seat John had occupied. He wasn't under arrest. Donaldson had given him an ultimatum. He could either come back to Waldport with him to "help him with his investigation" or Donaldson could get a warrant and have Portland police haul him out of his office in handcuffs and make a public show of extraditing him.

Concerned about his reputation, Devore had come quietly.

He was alone in the room at the moment. Julia hovered in the bullpen, where Donaldson and his two deputies conferred around Min's desk.

"Salem confirms John's story," Oliver said. "They found the report from the officer that responded to the hospital. Belle wouldn't talk to him but he did get both their names. And there's more. The hospital ran a rape kit on Belle. It never got tested. It's been in storage ever since."

"Go get it," Donaldson said. "Take it to Clackamas."

Oliver left and Donaldson tipped his head towards the door to the interrogation room and told Min, "you're with me. Take notes and handle the recorder. Don't say or do anything unless I tell you to."

She followed him into the room and Julia ducked in after.

Wayne Devore sat at the table with his hands folded in front of him. He gave the two deputies a hooded, resentful look.

He opened his mouth to speak but Donaldson forestalled him with a raised finger and nodded at Min. She put the tape recorder on the table and turned it on.

"Lieutenant Manfred Donaldson and Corporal Sarah Min conducting an interview with Wayne Devore," Donaldson said for the record, adding the date, time, and location. "Mr. Devore, for the record I'm going to read you your rights." He did so, then asked Devore if he wanted an attorney present.

"I don't need an attorney. I didn't do anything."

"It's a formality," Donaldson said. "I'm required to ask."

"Fine. You asked. Can we get on with this?"

"Certainly." Donaldson was carrying a file folder. He set it down and opened it, read something to himself, then closed it again. "We've brought you here to discuss the alleged rape of Annabelle Mary Lodge on the evening of Thursday, August 7, 1986. Now, of course, Oregon has a 12-year statute of limitations on prosecuting cases of rape. However, your involvement in this affair calls into question the possibility of your involvement in the murder of Lodge's sister-in-law, Julia Lodge. Murder, as I'm sure you know, doesn't have a statute of limitations."

Min was frowning but kept her mouth shut.

Donaldson folded his arms on the closed folder and leaned in. "So. You want to tell me what happened?"

"Nothing," Devore said. "Nothing happened." His gaze darted to the right. "And you'd have no way to prove it even if it did."

"Then you won't mind giving us a DNA sample."

Devore hesitated.

"I mean," Donaldson said, "if you're innocent and all..."

"Sure," Devore said. "Fine. Whatever."

Donaldson nodded to Min and they sat in silence while she left the room, returned with an evidence collection kit, and took a swab from inside Devore's cheek.

She put the swab into a labelled evidence bag, left the room with it, and returned without it a few seconds later.

"Well?" Donaldson asked.

"I got Oliver on the radio. He stopped to gas up his car

and hadn't left yet. He's going to pick it up and take it with him, so the lab can test it at the same time."

"The same time as what?" Devore demanded.

"Funny you should ask." Donaldson gave him a predatory smile. "Belle called her brother from a payphone outside a Gas-N-Gone station a few miles from Corvallis. We have the phone records." He took a sheet of paper out of his folder and laid it on the table. "He picked her up and took her to the emergency room in Salem, where he reported the rape to the city police." He took that report from the file and set it next to the phone records.

"That doesn't prove--"

"The hospital ran a rape kit on her. That kit and your DNA are on their way to the state crime lab at Clackamas right now."

All the blood drained from Devore's face.

"Do you maybe want to re-think your statement? Lying to the police is a crime all by itself, you know. I'd love to have something solid I could arrest you for."

Devore took a short, sharp breath. "I didn't have anything to do with Julia Lodge," he said.

Donaldson half rose from his seat, looming over the other man. "Tell me *what happened*," he demanded.

"Okay," Wayne Devore said, "but you're going to have to keep this confidential. People are...narrow-minded. Something like this could damage my reputation."

"I won't tell anyone who doesn't have a right to know," Donaldson promised.

"Okay," he said again. "Belle was a sweet girl, but she was strong-willed. Foolish. Her parents wanted her to settle down and get married. Find a good Catholic boy, like me, and be a proper wife and mother. They weren't unreasonable. They let her go to college and get a bachelor's degree. You'd think that would be enough. But she was determined to go on and get a master's and then a doctorate. Take a man's job away from some poor bastard who deserved it more and have a *career*. I decided to intervene, for her own good. Show her what can happen to willful young women who don't do as their elders tell them."

Min growled and half came out of her seat. Donaldson put a hand on her shoulder and pushed her down without looking at her.

"How did you get Belle alone and when?" he asked.

"She met me for coffee," he said. "She didn't really want to, but her parents convinced her. It was about two o'clock. Afterwards, I got her to walk me to my car. I just pushed her in from the driver's side and drove away. She tried to get out, but I drove too fast. I took her to a cabin I knew about, out in the woods, and...you know."

"Say it," Min demanded.

"What?"

"Say it!"

Devore looked between the two law officers. "Fine. I had sex with her. Look, I didn't do anything wrong. I was already planning to marry her. I just claimed my rights a little early."

"Had sex with her?" Min echoed, coming up and lunging over the table, causing him to cringe back. "Had sex with her? You didn't have sex with her, you miserable fuck. You didn't have any rights to claim. You raped her. You're a rapist, you worthless, sniveling piece of shit!"

Donaldson got her by the shoulder and eased her back into her chair. Devore looked from her to him.

"I'm here cooperating with you voluntarily," he said to Donaldson. "I don't appreciate being spoken to like this by your subordinate."

Donaldson nodded once, shortly, and leaned over to speak quietly and at length in Min's ear. She was trembling and breathing hard. When he fell silent she rose without a word and left the room.

Donaldson turned back to Devore. "I'm going to need to know where you went after you let Belle go. She made her call to her brother just after 7 PM. Corvallis is only an hour and a half from Waldport. Plenty of time for you to make a side trip. What about it? Did you decide you wanted to finish up with a little dark meat?"

"No. No! I swear. I told you, I went to San Francisco that

night."

"No, you told me you went to San Francisco that afternoon."

"I didn't drive. That was the only thing I wasn't candid about. My friends drove down. I flew down and met up with them at the hotel. Ask Earl Stanton. He'll tell you I did."

"Your buddy Stanton was already prepared to lie for you. Why should I believe him about this?"

"He thought he was covering for me in case Belle's parents found out we'd had sex. He didn't know she didn't want to. Talk to Earl. He'll tell you the truth."

"Mmm. Maybe." The recorder was still running. Donaldson was quiet for a minute, doodling on the cover of his file folder. "How did you convince her to marry you?

Devore half laughed. "I never asked her."

"I'm sorry?"

"She wouldn't tell me where she lived. I was only going to be a gentleman and take her home. So I asked her mother. Told her I wanted to send Belle flowers and she gave me the address. Then I just waited a couple of weeks and called her folks and asked them to meet us at her apartment. Told them we had something we wanted to tell them. I let them get there first, then I just went in behind them, put my arm around Belle's shoulders and told her parents she'd agreed to marry me. They were so happy, she couldn't refuse."

Julia lay her hand flat against the two-way mirror and concentrated on the energy binding the molecules together. It cracked side to side with a sound like a gunshot and the two men both flinched.

Donaldson shook his head, shuffled his papers back into their manila folder and stood up.

"Is someone going to give me a ride back to Portland?" Devore asked.

"Someone's going to give you a ride somewhere."

"And I'm going to hold you to your promise of confidentiality. If any word of this leaks, I will sue this department."

Donaldson laughed abruptly. "Yeah. Good luck with that."

The door opened and Min came back in with more papers. She set them on the table, circled behind Devore and handcuffed him ungently.

"What the-- Hey! What the hell are you doing?"

"Wayne Devore, you're under arrest for rape in the sexual assault of Annabelle Lodge and for second-degree manslaughter for your actions which led to her death."

"She killed herself. You can't arrest me for that! And the statute of limitation on rape ran out years ago."

"Oh," Donaldson said, "did I forget to mention the exception in cases where a rapist is identified using DNA evidence? The statute of limitations on that is two years."

"But--"

"Two years," Min said, "from when the DNA evidence is matched to a suspect's DNA. And second-degree manslaughter includes causing someone to commit suicide."

"What's the statute of limitations on that?"

"There isn't one. The Benton County Sheriff's Department is filing charges. We'll be holding you until they can extradite you for trial. Also, given the nature of your crimes and your position working with vulnerable young people, the Portland Police Department is getting a warrant to seize your home and office computers and any other electronics in your possession."

"You can't do that!"

"Watch me."

"You can call your attorney at any time," Donaldson said. "Have him meet you at the county jail. Deputy Min will be taking you there and processing you into the system now."

"Be sure to smile when we leave the office," Min said. "Word got out that there's been a development in the Lodge murder case and the parking lot is absolutely swarming with news media."

Chapter Twenty-Six

True Colors

[Cyndi Lauper, 1986]

When Min had left with Devore, the sheriff made a brief statement to the press. Afterwards he came back to the bullpen with Donaldson.

"It was good of you to let Min make the arrest," the sheriff said.

Donaldson shrugged. "I figured it would humiliate him more, being arrested by a woman."

"You think?"

"It would me."

"Oh." The sheriff shook his head. "So I suppose this puts us back at square one as far as the murder is concerned."

"No. No, not hardly."

"Really?"

Donaldson gave him a direct look. "This doesn't clear John Lodge, you know that, right?"

"No...How do you figure?"

"We know he was at Corvallis. That's only an hour and a half away from Waldport. If he *did* go back to Portland with Belle after they left the emergency room he likely wouldn't have had time to come here and kill Julia, but we only have his word that he did. And think about it. The Millers said Julia told them that she had a family emergency. We know now that that was true. She *did* have a family emergency. But no one knew that except for John, Belle, and Devore."

"What do you think happened?"

"I don't know. And I am going to follow up on Devore going to San Francisco. But if his alibi on that point holds, it all comes back to John again."

———❤———

People mispronounced "Williamette". They always had. But anyone from Oregon knew it was Will-AM-ette and not Will-yam-ETTE. The Williamette Valley, 150 miles long, followed the Williamette River, fed by mountain ranges on three sides. It stretched from Corvallis in the south, past the state capital of Salem, to Portland in the north. Beautiful and incredibly fertile, it was home to 70% of the state's population and was famous as the final destination along the historic Oregon Trail.

The Oregon Coastal Range separated it from the Pacific Ocean and anyone wanting to drive from Salem to Waldport had to either go north and take highway 30 along the Columbia River, follow narrow, dangerous highway 18 along the Salmon River through the Van Duzer Corridor to Lincoln City, or travel down to Corvallis and follow highway 20 west.

Donaldson had real, old-fashioned paper maps taped to the walls of the squadroom and he was tracing routes, color-coding them and taking notes.

"Did you ever hear of someone named Cool Papa Bell?" Min asked out of the blue.

He looked up. "Who?"

"Cool Papa Bell."

"I don't know. Who is he?"

"I don't know either. I've just had that name stuck in my head."

Ricky McFarlane, the K-9 officer was at his desk, Lando asleep on the carpet at his feet. He glanced up. "Did you google it?"

"No." Min sighed. "I guess that would be the smart thing to do, wouldn't it."

"Which probably explains why you didn't," Donaldson offered without looking up.

Min pulled out her phone and held it to her mouth. "Okay, Google," she said, "Cool Papa Bell."

A voice came out of the phone.

"Cool Papa Bell was a American baseball player who played centerfield in the Negro Leagues from 1922 to 1946. Considered by many to be one of the fastest men ever to play the game, he was inducted into the Hall of Fame in 1974."

"That is totally radical," Julia said "You all are not even impressed. Do you not understand how skip diggity all these gizmos are? You have libraries at your fingertips *all the time*."

"So what made you think of him?" McFarlane asked.

"I don't know. I just had his name stuck in my head." She read further on her phone, then stopped and looked up. Her expression was shaken.

"What is it?"

"Oh, it's nothing," she said, trying and failing to sound nonchalant. "It's just a weird coincidence."

"What is?"

"There's a link here to an old article about him in an historical society newspaper database."

"Yeah. And?"

"The article was written by a Rueben Meyers. Wasn't Julia's dad's name Rueben Myers? And he was a journalist, right?"

"Oooh," Donaldson mocked absentmindedly. "Spooky."

McFarlane rolled his eyes. "I'll let you in on a secret," he told Min. "I've worked my share of homicides. These weird little coincidences happen more often than you'd expect."

"Two hours," Donaldson said.

The other two turned to look at him.

"What?" Min asked.

"Two hours," he repeated. "While you've been playing Ghostbuster--"

("I know that movie!" Julia exclaimed.)

"--I've calculated that the fastest route Lodge could have taken from Salem to Waldport was just under two hours."

"That's what you've been doing all afternoon?" Min asked. "Because I could have just googled it..."

Donaldson made a face and opened his mouth but before he could speak the door swung inward and Oliver entered, looking down at his own phone. He glanced up and found Donaldson's gaze.

"Oh, hey. I just got off the phone with Portland PD. I've got some news for you."

"Yeah? What?"

Oliver chewed on his lower lip, tipped his head and half shrugged. You're not going to like it...."

——♥——

Rose Meyer still lived in the house on West Broadway in Eugene. Julia had grown up there and knew it better than any other corner of the Earth, but even here the 21st century had brought changes. The red cedar tree was gone from the front yard, not even a stump to show where it had been. A big, flat screen television was mounted on a wall in the living room, a laptop computer sat open on the coffee table and one of the ubiquitous smart phones was charging on the stand that had held, in Julia's life, a black rotary phone.

She followed Donaldson and her mother into the kitchen and sighed aloud at the sight of her mother's coffee pot, the same aluminum percolator she'd had since before Julia was born, sitting in its familiar place on the back right burner. It was a simple metal pot with a black plastic handle. Inside, a strainer basket held coffee grounds at the top of a hollow metal stand. A hollow glass knob on the lid allowed you to see the bubbling coffee, to judge when it was ready to drink.

Julia had scrubbed it a thousand times. It had been the first hot thing she'd been allowed to hold. She'd drunk her first cup of coffee from it. Made her first pot of coffee in it.

She felt, not for the first time, that she was trapped in a dream world. Everything was so familiar. Everything was so strange.

Rose motioned Donaldson to a seat at the table, poured out two cups of coffee and took the chair across from him. He took a sip and gave her a smile that didn't reach his eyes.

"Your coffee is strong and black. Like you."

Julia rolled her eyes.

Rose peered at him over the rim of her own cup, lips pursed and one eyebrow raised. "Just tell me why you're here," she said.

He sighed, set down his cup and folded his arms on the table.

"John Lodge's alibi is solid. He isn't the one who killed your daughter."

"I see."

"The night that Julia disappeared, John went to Corvallis to pick up his sister and took her to an emergency room in Salem after she called to tell him that she'd been raped."

"I know this. It was on the news three nights ago. Why are you coming here to me today?"

Donaldson sat back, ran a hand through his hair and blew out a breath.

"I still thought he was the best suspect. He left Portland just after seven and called the Salem police from the emergency room just before ten. The police report shows that an officer talked to him and Belle in the ER waiting room about a quarter to eleven. A second officer picked up the rape kit from the hospital just before 3:00 AM and spoke briefly with both of the Lodges. So we know he didn't have time to get to Waldport before about five in the morning. That would tie in with the approximate time that the Millers said Julia left Jude with them, and they said Julia told them there was a family emergency, which we know now there was. Only John and Belle knew that at the time, though."

"That makes sense," Rose agreed. "So why have you changed your mind?"

He made a face. "John's claim that he took his sister back home to Portland after they left the emergency room has been unexpectedly proven to be true. A woman by the name of Isadora Langthorpe contacted the Portland Police Department after the story about John's alibi ran on TV the other night."

"And she just happens to remember something that happened more than thirty years ago? And you believe her?"

"Not exactly. Her maiden name was Isadora Mayfield. She lived across the street from your daughter and a couple of houses down."

"We called her Izzy, Mom," Julia offered. "Squirrelly little teenager with the frizzy red hair and all those freckles. I know you met her."

"Oh, I think maybe I knew her," Rose said. "Everyone called her Izzy. She had freckles--lots of them. She was always trying strange things to get rid of them, like rubbing lemon rinds on her face or drinking pickle juice. Julia used to giggle about it and feel bad for her at the same time."

"Yes, I imagine that was her."

"And what did she tell you that makes you dismiss John as a suspect?"

"August 8, 1986, was Izzy's sixteenth birthday. Her parents surprised her with a car. They had it parked on a church parking lot a couple of blocks away and very early that morning her dad walked over and drove it home. Then he and her mother decorated it with ribbons and bows and took a picture, to commemorate the event."

He reached into his breast pocket and took out an old photo printed in color on plain typing paper.

"This was taken facing to the southeast. You can see, the sky is just beginning to lighten. Sunrise in Portland on August 8 is 6:01 AM, so this picture was taken between 5:30 and 6:00."

Rose took the picture and studied it. Julia had already seen it, when Oliver printed it off his computer after taking the phone call from the Portland police. It showed Izzy's new car, wrapped in ribbons and with a giant red bow on top, parked next to the curb in front of her house.

In the background, partially obscured by a lilac bush but clear enough to identify, John's car sat in the Lodge's driveway.

"So that's that," Donaldson said. "There's no way he could have gone from Salem to Waldport and back to Portland in less than three hours, let alone have time to kill Julia, dispose of her body, and get rid of her car."

"You see?" Julia couldn't help but say. "You doubted me. You thought I was wrong about John and got myself killed for it. But I wasn't. I was right all along."

"He still should have told me," Rose said stubbornly. "My daughter was missing. I had a *right* to know what was going on. And we were supposed to be family. I'd have helped him. Didn't he know that? I'd have helped him take care of Belle. We could have given the poor thing the support she needed before--" She broke off and stood abruptly, went to the sink. She dumped the rest of her coffee, rinsed the cup and set it in the strainer and stood for a long minute looking out the back window into the garden.

She still wasn't crying, but her eyes were damp and she dashed a hand across them angrily.

"Still. It must have been very lonely for the Lodge children. Dealing with a thing like that and you can't even go to your own momma." She came back to the table and settled into her chair. "So where do we go from here?"

Donaldson was caught in the middle of taking a drink of coffee. He choked a little and set the cup down.

"We don't go anywhere. He didn't do it. I'm not saying I like John Lodge, or approve of him keeping quiet for so long, but I can't arrest him for something I know he's innocent of."

"I wasn't suggesting you should. Mister Donaldson, are you under the impression that my sole objective is to see John in prison?"

"Well...you've certainly said as much on more than one occasion."

"I believed that he killed my daughter. He didn't. Okay, but someone did. What are you going to do about catching them?"

"I...ah..."

Rose gave him a look of withering disapproval. It was an expression Julia knew well and the intervening years had not robbed it of one iota of its power.

"I hope you didn't come here expecting a pat on the head and a little plastic trophy that says, 'I tried'. My daughter's killer is still out there, *Mister* Donaldson. I expect you to find that person and put them in prison, where they belong. After all, I'm given to understand that justice is your business."

Chapter Twenty-Seven

Rock Me Amadeus

[Falco, 1985]

"Hit me again."

The bartender swiped a less-than-clean rag across the wood. "Not sure that's such a good idea, pal."

Donaldson rapped his glass on the bar. "I said hit me again!"

"Look, buddy, I'd like to help you out, but you've had quite a few already. Hey! How about a cup of coffee instead? On the house."

"I don't want y'goddamn coffee. I want you to hit me again."

"Look, if you wanna drink yourself to death, that's your business." The guy's nametag said "Ted". He was probably six-five, close to three hundred pounds, with a tattoo of a dragon on his left arm and a lumberjack beard. "But if I serve you when you're this far gone, I could lose my license."

Donaldson fished his badge out of his pocket and slapped it on the bar. "I start paying attention to how many seventeen-year-old girls you serve in the back room on a Friday night, you could lose a lot more than your license." He rapped the glass angrily against the wood. "Hit me a-fucking-gain!"

Ted looked around nervously. It was a weeknight and the bar was nearly deserted. Two young couples were playing pool in the far corner and a solitary old man nursed a beer at a booth by the jukebox. Ted reached for the scotch.

"Fine. Don't blame me when you're dead."

Julia twirled on the next barstool over. "Look at you,

drinking yourself into a stupor because you're scared of my momma."

Donaldson looked right at her. "Oh, shut up. Nobody asked you."

She nearly fell off the barstool in shock. "You can see me?"

"Don't let it go to your head," he said. "There are space aliens swimming in the vodka and that stuffed moose over there keeps telling me dirty jokes."

"Okay, but I'm real."

"Sure you are."

Ted slid the whisky across the bar and walked away muttering "fuck my life."

"How about if I can prove it to you?"

"How?"

Julia slid off the barstool and went to the jukebox. Holding onto things was still a problem, but she was getting good at moving them. She reached into the machine and moved the lever that would normally be triggered by quarters and it invited her to choose a song. She studied the list. Most of them were unfamiliar titles by strange bands but she saw a familiar name and punched in the code for it.

When she turned, the old man with the beer was staring through her at the juke box, eyes wide and wondering. "Hey, Ted," he called. "Is that thing supposed to do that?"

Ted came over to him. "Is what supposed to do what?"

"The juke box. It just punched its own buttons."

"You must be imagining things."

Before he had finished speaking a swell of music came from the speakers and Madonna's singing filled the small bar.

"When you call my name, it's like a little prayer..."

"Yeah, that ain't creepy at all," Ted said.

Julia returned to her barstool. "You see?" she demanded.

Donaldson took a slug of whisky and shrugged. "Okay, fine. You're real. So what?"

"So what are you going to do about finding out who killed me?"

"If you're real, why don't you just tell me who killed you?"

"*I don't know!*"

"Huh." He snorted. "That figures. Useless bitch."

"You're the cop. Figure it out."

"I got no idea."

"Well maybe you would have, if you hadn't spent the last thirty-odd years trying to frame my husband."

He turned on her, angry. "Listen, I never tried to frame anybody. I'm a good cop. I know you don't like me, but I'm a good cop and I do my damn job."

"Uh, who are you talking to?" Ted asked.

"None of your business," Donaldson shot at him. "Hey, did you serve the lady?" He turned back to Julia. "You want something to drink?"

"I don't think I *can* drink. I'm dead, remember?"

"Oh." He gave Ted his attention again. "Never mind. She's dead."

"Right. I'm just gonna...go down to the other end of the bar and...stay there."

Donaldson turned his attention to his own reflection, rumpled and red-eyed, in the mirror above the bar. "Fuck his life," he muttered. "Huh. Fuck *my* life."

"I brought Jude to Waldport," Julia persisted. "I took him berrying. We played on the beach and went to sleep. That's all I know. I don't remember waking up that night. I don't remember anyone coming for me, or taking him to the Miller's. I didn't know about Belle. What happened to me, Donaldson? Why am I dead?"

"I don't know," he snapped. "And to be honest, I don't really give a damn."

"Oh that's nice. What ever happened to," she lowered her voice mockingly, "'justice is my business'? Or is justice only your business when it means you can attack my husband?"

"I thought he was guilty. He acted guilty. I do have standards. I would never knowingly put an innocent person behind bars."

"That didn't stop you from arresting me."

"I apologized for that."

"After you were forced to. You make snap judgements about people and want to believe you're magically right. And when you hurt someone who doesn't deserve it, when you hound them and humiliate them, you just shrug it off and say you were doing your job. You know, I know why you're doing this."

"Doing what?"

"This. This pity party. Drinking yourself into a stupor." She leaned in close, getting right in his face. "You wanted John to be guilty. You wanted him to be guilty because you thought that somehow that would exonerate you. You weren't *really* a racist bastard. You were just a good cop who was *misunderstood*."

Donaldson turned on her and raised his voice, flinging his arms around and sending his nearly-empty glass flying. "I just don't want to be the asshole. Everybody always calls me an asshole. You called me that. Your husband called me that, the media called me that, my ex-wife calls me that. Hell. Even my own goddamn kid calls me that. For thirty years I've been the asshole. I'm tired of always being the asshole, okay?"

"Then stop being an asshole. Why is this hard for you?"

"Why don't you just go to," he paused for half a second, "heaven?" he bellowed. "Or hell, for all I care. Or wherever it is that dead people go? Just go away and leave me alone."

The bar was humming with energy. Power ran through the juke box. Through the neon signs and the light dangling over the pool table. The people in the room were all staring at Donaldson and the air thrummed with their emotions: unease and amusement and curiosity. Julia could feel it and smell it and taste it. She pulled it all in and channeled it into her fury. A line of glasses hanging over the bar shivered and clinked together.

"Because I want justice," she screamed.

Static electricity crackled around her. Her hair rose as if in a storm wind. The room grew cold. The tap on the beer flew off and an amber geyser shot up behind the bar.

"You promised me justice."

A bottle of rum exploded with a sound like a rifle shot, and then a bottle of bourbon. The bar mirror fogged up and cracked from side to side.

"You owe me justice, God damn it! You get me justice!"

Chapter Twenty-Eight

Train of Thought

[A-Ha, 1985]

"Did I throw up in your car last night?"

Min made a face. "Yeah, you did."

"Huh." Donaldson shrugged. "Good."

"Good?" she stared at him. "It's good that you threw up in my car?"

"Better than throwing up in my car. Where is my car, by the way? I had to get a taxi this morning. And how did you find me?"

"The bartender called me. I don't know what you did but he was really freaked out. Your car's probably still wherever you parked it last night."

Donaldson was back in his office. Julia sat on the floor in the corner, feeling hungover herself. He could no longer hear her and didn't seem to remember anything that had happened. Their fight had left her drained and exhausted and she carefully drew small amounts of power from the electronics in the room the way that, in life, she'd have sipped coffee.

"What now?" Min asked. "Where do we go from here?"

"We start over. Back to square one. Have you been watching the tip line? Anything there?"

"A lot of responses. Most of them probably don't amount to anything, honestly," Min said. "People all over the country who think they saw Julia alive days or weeks or even years after she disappeared. A few kooks."

"Define kooks?"

"Couple of psychics offering to channel her or claiming

they've been visited by her spirit. A guy who says if we have a suspect he can check their auras to see if they're guilty. And I had a really spooky conversation with a really nice lady who claims she saw Julia's ghost on the beach behind the beach house where she was staying back in the mid-nineties, when she was a little girl. She said Julia was wearing a nightshirt and looking for her son."

Julia looked up. "Emma Grace! It has to be. Little Emma Grace, all grown up. Wow." She frowned and shook her head. "There's a lot of that going around," she commented drily.

"Now there's a thought," Donaldson said.

"What? Contacting her ghost?"

He gave the young deputy a withering look. "The Millers never did say what she was wearing."

"Is that surprising? The Millers were high and half asleep."

"No, but if we could figure out what she was wearing when she disappeared, it might tell us where she was going."

"Okay, that makes sense. But how?"

Oliver came in looking at his phone. "I've got a report from the university on the forensic biology from Julia's car."

"Yeah? And?"

"When the car went into the ravine it crushed some saplings. They did tree ring dating on the wood from the stumps and it shows they were broken off in 1986. They were also able to analyze the mix of pollen and spores that were trapped inside the car the last time the door was closed and that gave them specific data about the time of year. They think it was dumped within a week of the night Julia disappeared."

"She was killed that night," Donaldson said. "The storm the next night would have made it too dangerous to go out in a boat and dump a body, but it was the only storm that summer strong enough to push her all the way into the cave and up out of reach of the tide."

"Like I said," Oliver persisted. "So I was right."

"Don't let it go to your head."

"So what do we do now?"

"We try to figure out what she was wearing. There was

nothing with her body to suggest clothing. No zippers or buckles, no buttons, although plastic buttons could very well have been washed away. We don't even know if she was wearing anything when her body was dumped. The body could have been naked, especially if she was raped first. But she wasn't naked when she went with her killer up to leave Jude at the Millers."

"So how do we do that?" Min asked again. "And what will it tell us if we do?"

Donaldson chose to take the second question first. "It might tell us something about the person who came for her and the circumstances. Did she take time to get dressed? Did she just throw something on over her nightgown? Did he drag her out of the house without letting her change?" He looked at Min and Oliver and read the skepticism on their faces. "Okay, yes. I'm catching at straws. When all you have are straws, that's what you do. Do either of you have a better idea?"

They both shook their heads.

"But how do we figure out what she was wearing?" Min persisted.

"You tell me."

She thought about it. "We have all her clothes," she realized. "You seized them when you searched the Lodge's house and they've been in evidence ever since. So we could...ask her family what's missing?"

"We can do that. They might not be able to tell us. But there's another possibility. I want you to get together every picture you can find of Julia Lodge from the summer of 1986."

"Right! We can compare what she's wearing to what we still have."

"If someone was stalking her," Oliver suggested, "maybe he'll turn up in some of the pictures. We should look for the same person in the background of multiple photographs, especially ones taken at different times and in different places."

"Good idea," Donaldson conceded with unusual generosity. "Why don't *you* contact Rose Meyers and get any pictures she has. Have her connect you with anyone else in the family who might have pictures as well. There are some aunts and cousins on that side. And *you*," he turned to Min, "can get ahold of John and Jude and get anything they've got. And find out what became of the Lodge's property after Muriel died."

"You don't think they'd have had pictures of Julia, do you?" Min asked. "I gather they didn't spend much time together. I don't think they liked her, nor her them."

"No, but they probably wound up with Belle's belongings and Belle was John and Julia's closest friend. If anyone had pictures of Julia, she did."

———♥———

Julia had it down to a science now, how close she could get to various electronic devices before her presence affected their performance. Oliver was at his desk, engrossed in staring down at his phone.

If she haunted this place for a million years, Julia would never get over the technological advances that had been made since her death. In her day even truly long-distance phone calls had been complicated. She remembered watching some special on television, during the summit between Reagan and Gorbachev, that involved a telephone conversation in real time with some person or group in Moscow. It was an awkward segment because there was a several second delay each time someone spoke, while they waited for the sound to travel.

Now they could not only speak normally, they could instantly trade text, pictures, even videos. She'd seen McFarlane playing games on his phone and overheard Min talking to her grandmother in Seoul. Oliver had finished a conversation with Julia's own mother not ten minutes earlier, which wouldn't have seemed out of the ordinary except that he was now "unzipping" a "file" she had "emailed" him containing pictures of Julia that she had "scanned in" years ago.

Julia had had a fancy new cordless phone. John had bought it for them earlier that summer and they were still playing with it when she died, experimenting with how far from the base they could get and giggling over taking it into the bathroom and talking to people from the back yard.

She imagined, briefly, sitting for hours with it in her lap, staring down at it, and suppressed a half-hysterical laugh.

The police were trying, she'd give Donaldson that, but it didn't seem to her like they were accomplishing a damned thing.

Donaldson came out of his office.

"Where are we?"

Oliver looked up. "Rose Meyers just sent me a file full of pictures of Julia. I'm going to run them through a facial recognition program and see if anyone pops up repeatedly that we wouldn't expect. Hell, someone might have been stalking Julia for weeks or months, just waiting for a chance to get her alone."

"Okay. Any word from Min?"

"She had to drive up to Portland to pick something up. Gonna be pretty late before she gets back."

"Okay, well, we might as well knock off for the day. After you get that program running. Give me a ride?" It was half a demand and half a request, which surprised Julia a little.

"Sure. Just don't be puking in my ride. That was really gross last night."

"Yeah, whatever. Don't start with me."

"Just saying. Where do you need to go?"

"Wherever the hell I left my car."

Oliver switched from his phone to his laptop computer, fiddled with it for a few minutes, then closed it down and stood up. "It's running. Maybe it'll have something for us by morning."

Donaldson nodded, went back and turned his office light out and closed the door. He raked his gaze around the squad room and it seemed to Julia that they rested on her for a second, but he moved on and made no mention of it. He did say to Oliver, though, as she followed the two men from the building, "I had the damndest dream last night..."

———♥———

"Muriel Lodge was a bitch."

"Atta girl." Julia would have given Min a high five if she were corporeal.

"Probably," Donaldson agreed. "What led you to that conclusion?"

The young deputy had come in carrying a white cardboard carton and she'd set it careful on her desk before making her abrupt proclamation.

"I realize she was grieving. Her daughter had just killed herself. But she and her husband cut John *and Jude* out of their lives completely right after the funeral. And she literally cut them out of Belle's pictures. The two of them and Julia and all Belle's friends from college. When she died--Muriel--she left everything to the church. One of the sisters contacted John and let him take whatever he wanted. All that's left is sliced up pictures of Belle by herself, with her parents, members of the church, and Devore. Lots of pictures of her and Devore. From the look of them, her mother made her pose for them. Poor baby looks miserable. How Muriel didn't see what she was doing to that poor child I will never understand."

Julia, with tears in her eyes, looked at Min with affection. "Bless your heart," she said. "You know she was about the same age you are, right?"

"So no luck?"

"Not with that. No. But maybe with this. I didn't look at it. I figured we'd open it here."

She took the lid off the box and the two men moved in.

"What is it?" Donaldson demanded but Julia recognized it as soon as Min lifted it free.

"Her book bag. I gave her that." It was blue like the ocean, covered in whales and dolphins and rainbows. When she'd seen it in the store, Julia had thought of her sister-in-law immediately.

"After Julia disappeared, Belle spent a lot of time with John and Jude. She was responsible for organizing a lot of the search efforts. She kept all her notes and supplies in here. After she died, John found it on the back floorboard of his car. He's never opened it, but he's kept it ever since."

"So let's see what she had."

The first thing Min pulled out of the bag was a stack of missing person posters. "She must have designed these. You know, I still see them around town at some of the older businesses?"

Julia had seen them, too. One of them, anyway, staring

back at her from inside the dark and long-abandoned Zoosie's. She imagined Belle, mocking them up. Choosing the picture and the font to use, getting them copied and going from store to store asking to put them up. Realizing the love that had gone into this both warmed her heart and broke it.

Min emptied the rest of the book bag onto her desk. There were index cards and colored pencils and large-scale topographical maps of the Waldport area with search patterns marked on it and crossed out, each X neatly cross-referenced with a date and time.

Oliver snagged one of the maps and studied it. "They came within about a quarter mile of finding Julia's car," he said with a shake of his head.

The last item in the book bag was Belle's Trapper Keeper, something so familiar to Julia it tore at her heart. It was blue with a Lisa Frank design of purple dolphins and a peace sign Belle herself had outlined with tiny prisms. Min opened it.

"It looks like she kept a search journal."

She'd written on regular college-lined notebook paper. It was so odd to see her familiar handwriting in faded ink on paper grown yellow with age and realize how many years had passed since she set down her pen for the last time.

"Okay," Donaldson said, "Let's split them up and see what she had to say."

Min opened the three ring binder and divided the pages among the three of them. Donaldson and Oliver snagged chairs and they sat down and read. Julia flitted around the desk, trying to see over their shoulders.

Oliver broke the silence first.

"Fuck," he said.

The other two looked up. "What?"

He shook his head and read aloud. "John hasn't said anything yet. Maybe it hasn't occurred to him, but I'm sure it will. He was on his way here when I called him. If I hadn't distracted him, he'd have been here. This is my fault."

Julia sank down on the corner of the desk. "Oh, baby. I should have ripped that bastard's heart out when I had the chance."

Min surreptitiously dabbed at the corner of her eye and cleared her throat. "Belle started her own investigation. I have diagrams of the beach and the surrounding area. She's got names and home addresses for everyone who was staying in the other beach houses and notes from when she questioned them."

"Now that could be something." Donaldson held out his hand and Min surrendered some, but not all, of the papers she was holding. He looked them over. "She was pretty thorough."

"Of course she was," Julia said. "That was Belle."

"Okay, the Lodge's beach house was the last one in the line at the end of the road, before the Miller's place. The house next to them was empty that night. It was rented by a couple of college kids who went to a party in town and wound up spending the night in the drunk tank. Here," he handed a page off to Oliver, "that's their names. You want to confirm the alibi?"

"I'm on it." Oliver returned to his own desk.

"The next house over was a family and they heard something."

Min stilled and looked up and Oliver, busy with his computer kept one eye on Donaldson.

"They were sitting up playing cards, waiting for their oldest son to show up and they remembered hearing a noise, but they couldn't say for sure where it came from. The kid thought it was a gunshot but his father, who was an Army vet, said no. He thought it was a screen door slamming or maybe a car door. But, get this, no cars had driven down the street that night."

"They were sure of that?" Oliver asked, returning. "The alibis check out," he added as an aside. "They were both picked up for public intoxication and released the next day."

"They were sure," Donaldson confirmed. "Remember, they were up because they were waiting for someone."

Oliver picked his share of the journal back up and the three returned to reading.

"This is odd," he commented after a few minutes.

"Would you like to share with the class?"

He glanced to Donaldson. "Julia's pillows were gone."

"Her pillows?"

"Yeah. Belle says here that Julia always took their good things with them on vacation. Good china and fine linens."

"That's stupid."

"Oh, screw you," Julia told him.

"Apparently her reasoning was that, if there's ever a time for luxury, it's when you're on vacation. She had a set of really nice pillows that should have been on the bed there, but they weren't. John said he didn't know what to make of it. Belle was afraid someone had used them to suffocate her, but she didn't want to suggest that to John and she couldn't get any cops to listen to her."

"She didn't come to me."

"She says she did," Oliver told him, raising his eyebrows and looking at his boss sideways.

"Well, I don't remember it."

"It doesn't make any sense, though," Min said. "We know she wasn't suffocated. She died of blunt force trauma. Why would someone take her pillows?"

"They were nice pillows. Maybe the killer just took a liking to them," Donaldson suggested. The other two shrugged and they continued reading.

This time it was Min who drew their attention. She made a choking sound and when they looked over she was openly crying.

Donaldson's mouth twisted impatiently. "What is it?"

"The last entry," she said. "Eleven-fifteen AM, February 13, 1986."

"The day she killed herself," Oliver said softly. "What does it say?"

She slid the paper into the middle of the desk, turning it so they could read it for themselves. There was just one line, the writing heavy and uncharacteristically jagged.

It said, "I can't do this anymore."

——♥——

ODonaldson closed the door and locked it. He drew the blinds and turned off the overhead light and for a long time he sat kicked back in his chair with his feet on his desk and his eyes closed. If it hadn't been for the lack of snoring, she'd have thought he was asleep.

Finally he roused himself and left the room. When he returned he had a cup of coffee and he turned the light back on and pulled out a blank sheet of paper and a pen.

"What we know about the killer," he wrote.

"1. The killer knew where Julia was and probably knew she was alone (except Jude).

"2. Allowed her to take Jude to safety before he killed her.

"3. Knew where to hit her to destroy brain stem? (Luck?)

"4. Had some other means of transportation OR was local?

"5. Had somewhere to take her to kill her OR took her back to beach house?"

He threw down his pen in disgust. The evidence cartons with everything from the beach house were still sitting in the corner and Donaldson carried them over and set them on his desk and the table Min had been working at. The case file was on his desk and he rifled through it until he found an inventory of what was in the cartons. He read it, then read it again, then opened boxes until he found the ones with Julia's clothes in them and took everything out.

"No nightgown," he said to himself. "No blood on anything. No obvious weapon. No sign of a struggle. But no nightgown."

He went back to the list, studying it for a good half hour before he suddenly frowned and stood up. He pulled open the cartons again, one after another, searching.

"What is it?" Julia asked. "What are you looking for?"

If he could still hear her at all, he was ignoring her. He found Jude's bedding, the twin sheet set still pristine because Julia had never even put it on the bed in the smaller bedroom. His child-sized pillow looked sad and forgotten and the quilt Belle had made him stirred an ache in Julia's heart.

He used his penknife to make a small slit in the pillow casing. A few feathers tumbled out and Donaldson nodded, then took a single feather and carried it out into the squad room.

Julia followed, curious.

"Anybody got a lighter?" Donaldson asked.

One of the other cops produced a cigarette lighter and Donaldson, eyes wide, set the feather alight. As it burned down to his fingers, he dropped it and stepped on it to put it out, nodding to himself while the rest of the officers looked at him like he was crazy.

Already headed for the door, he pulled out his phone and hit a few buttons. Min answered and a few seconds later Oliver echoed her "hello."

"Stop whatever you're doing and get back here," Donaldson said. "I know who did it."

Chapter Twenty-Nine

Kyrie

[Mr. Mister, 1985]

The Miller property looked abandoned and unkempt. The mailbox at the foot of the driveway was open, the door hanging and the interior stuffed with uncollected envelopes and circulars. The grass grew long in the front yard. It swayed in a wind from the sea and a loose section of gutter dangled from the side of the house and creaked abysmally as it twisted and turned.

A reddish-orange Volkswagen Jetta was parked in front of the porch. Donaldson came to a stop behind it and threw himself from the car too quickly for Julia to follow. She dove through the steel and fiberglass door, like reaching into a solid object but on a larger scale, and caught up to the detective as he was pounding on the front door.

A stranger answered, a chubby, middle-aged woman in slacks and a floral blouse. She held a phone in her left hand and peered at Donaldson anxiously.

"Harriet isn't here," she said. "She went to the store. I've called her and she's on her way back." She indicated the phone.

Donaldson shrugged off the information. "I need to talk to Charlie Miller," he said, pushing his way into the living room.

The woman caught at his arm. "You can't. He's dying."

"Yeah, I figured that out a long time ago."

"No, you don't understand," she insisted. "He's dying. *Right now.*"

Donaldson froze and stared at her for the space of two seconds. "Then I really need to talk to him," he said, brushed her aside and headed for the bedroom.

The room was stuffy with the window closed, too warm, the air cloying with the scents of dust and medicine and a hint of urine. In spite of the heat, the old man lay on his back beneath a pile of covers, his head propped up on a thick pillow.

Something whined and whimpered. It moved near his right hip and Julia realized his little dog lay next to him, head burrowed against his hand, crying piteously.

"He took a sudden turn for the worse," the woman said softly, coming up behind Donaldson. "I'm trying to get him to hang on until his wife gets back, so that she can say goodbye."

"And you are?"

"Jasmine Hopkins. I'm with hospice."

Donaldson flashed her his badge without taking his eyes off Charlie. "I need to question him."

Jasmine stared at him, disbelieving. "Seriously?"

Donaldson ignored her and stepped forward. Charlie was breathing in long, deep, painful gasps and Julia could see a purple light beginning to gather around the edges of the room. A faint mist had begun to rise from his body. It reminded her of heatwaves off a pavement on a long ago summer day. Still, when Donaldson stepped into his field of vision, the old man's eyes were lucid.

"I know, Charlie," Donaldson said.

Charlie writhed and drew in a deep, struggling breath. He made an agonized choking noise that turned into a sob.

"I wouldn'ta said," he gasped. "I swear to God. If I'd known...I'd never...I'd never a said."

"I don't understand."

"Harry. I told 'er. I shouldn'ta said. Didn't know..."

"Wait." Donaldson shook his head in disgust and disbelief. "Are you trying to tell me it was *Harriet*?"

Charlie lay there silent for a long time, shaking with the effort of speaking. He blinked and tears ran down either side of his face. The little dog whimpered and he patted it awkwardly.

"Woke me up in the middle of the night, holdin' the boy."

"Jude? She was holding Jude?"

"Sleeping like an angel, his momma's blood on his face and in his hair an' she said..."

He broke off, wheezing and shuddering. Donaldson moved in close, getting right in his face.

"She said what, Charlie? What did she say?"

"She said, 'I done a terrible thing, but you have to forgive me 'cause I did it for you.'"

"I don't understand," Donaldson persisted. "Why did Julia Lodge have to die?"

The hospice worker, finally catching on, gasped. Both men ignored her.

"Mushrooms," Charlie said. "Found me in the woods. Saw me with the mushrooms."

"You're not making sense."

From Julia's vantage point she could see that the mist coming from him was stronger, but instead of rising it was pooling around his body. It was as if he was physically clinging to life so that he could finally talk.

From some inner reserve he found a burst of strength, reached up with both hands and caught at Donaldson's jacket. His whole body shook with the effort and the passion of his words.

"Don't take advantage of others' misfortunes," he said, looking Donaldson in the eye. "Ain't no good can ever come of it."

He let go and fell back onto the bed and mist rose around him like a dust cloud. His eyes closed and the light from his body became a steady thread, slowly unspooling to weave itself into a new form above where he lay.

"Mushrooms?" Donaldson demanded. "Mushrooms? What the hell are you talking about? Charlie? Talk to me!" He got him by the shoulders and shook him, but the old man was unconscious now, clearly beyond speech.

Donaldson looked a question at the hospice worker and she tipped her palms up and shook her head. "He's dying," she said. "It doesn't mean anything. It can't mean anything. He doesn't know what he's saying. You *can't* think the Millers had anything to do with that lady's death. They wouldn't! Not either of them. They're just this sweet old couple, that's all."

"No, it was them," Donaldson said. "It had to be them. It's the only thing that makes any sense. And the pieces fit. Except...except I don't know why they only killed Julia. If Jude had gone as well, everyone would have believed she took him and left. Even her husband would have believed it. The only thing that made her disappearance suspicious was that she never would have left her son. So why spare Jude?"

"Oh, but he was such a *sweet* little boy."

Donaldson turned slowly and the hospice lady looked up and screamed. Harriet Miller had come into the room unnoticed and she stood behind them in the doorway now holding a small silver handgun, the barrel pointed straight at Donaldson's back.

He tensed and held his hands out to his sides, palms up. She nodded approvingly and took a step but then he moved slightly and she flinched and pulled the trigger. The shot echoed in the small room, the sound mixing with Jasmine Hopkin's shriek and the jangled cacophony of a lamp shattering.

"Detective," Harriet said solemnly, "I'm an old woman with nothing left to lose. You really don't want to do anything stupid right now."

"I'm not doing anything," he assured her, hands still up.

Julia could see the muscles in his back trembling. The room shivered with tension. She could almost see it in the air and she drank it in like Rex had told her to. A feeling of power washed over her and all her senses heightened. She could smell the sea, hear the dog panting, see into all the solid objects without even trying.

The magazine at the base of the gun was filled with shadowy bullets. The spent cartridge had ejected and another bullet was already in place.

"I'm going to need you to step away from my husband," Harriet told Donaldson. "Move slowly. Keep your hands where I can see them and take a seat in that chair."

Donaldson did as he was told. When he was safely seated in the armchair at the foot of the bed, Harriet came in and backed up by the headboard, never taking her eyes or gun from him. She sat down next to the pillow. Charlie was on her right side and she held the gun in her right hand, but she reached over to capture his left hand in her own and pulled it into her lap. Throughout the whole process the barrel of her gun never wavered.

The hospice worker huddled in the far corner, weeping, and Harriet addressed her without looking away from Donaldson.

"Jasmine, you made me a promise. Tell me you still intend to keep it."

"What promise?" Donaldson demanded. He looked to the other woman. "What does she want you to do?"

"The dog," Jasmine said, forcing the words out between the tears. Julia could feel her terror. "I promised her I'd take care of the dog."

"And you still will?" Harriet demanded.

"Yes. Yes, I promise I will!"

"Best take her now, then," Harriet said. "Take her and go. Go around behind the detective when you leave." She spared her a brief glance. "I'm sorry," she said. "Sorry you got tangled up in this. I do appreciate everything you've done for us."

Jasmine shot Donaldson a questioning look and he nodded. She moved in hesitantly and snatched up the dog. It yelped, startled. She cuddled it and spoke soft nonsense in its ear and it burrowed into her arms as she edged around behind Donaldson and left the bedroom. Donaldson and Harriet sat in a silence broken only by Charlie's labored breathing until the outer door had closed behind her.

"Now what?" Donaldson asked.

Harriet petted Charlie's hand and ran a thumb across his wedding ring.

"If you have any questions," she said, "you'd best ask them now."

"What did Julia Lodge do?" he asked. "Why did you hate her so much?"

"I didn't hate her," Harriet objected immediately. "I never

hated her at all, poor thing. I was sorry for her. She just...she got in the way. Like that poor deer that got hit by the car. She got in the way and I had to put her down. I didn't want to. I didn't have a choice."

"I don't understand."

"Neither do I," Julia said.

The light pouring off Charlie had formed an astral body above him but unlike the deer it wasn't a double of his living form, or at least of his current living form. It was a young man with short hair and a firm jaw. His limbs were straight and his hands, resting at his sides, smooth and not knotted with arthritis like Charlie's. He wore overalls over a flannel shirt and a pair of boots and Julia wondered how many years it had been since Charlie had looked like this in life.

A thread still connected it to the old man's living form and neither moved.

"Poor Charlie," Harriet mused. "This would all have been so much simpler if he'd just let me tell you it was her husband who came and got her. You wanted so badly to put him in jail, and then we wouldn't have ever had to worry about anyone finding out. Charlie wouldn't have it, though. He felt sorry for the man. It bothered him, what I did, you know?"

"No shit," Donaldson replied, wonder in his voice.

"He stopped gathering mushrooms after that. Wouldn't even eat them, and he'd always loved them. I regretted that."

"You keep talking about mushrooms. What the hell do mushrooms have to do with anything?"

Harriet stared at him. "They have everything to do with it. Julia took her little boy into the woods to look for blackberries. They got lost and wandered onto our property. They ran into Charlie in the woods and they saw the mushrooms he'd picked."

"So?"

She sighed. "Do you have some way of recording this?" she asked him. "I'm only going to tell this story once."

"I have a recording app on my phone," he said. "I'll have to reach into my pocket to get it."

"Which pocket?"

He indicated his left breast pocket. He was telling the truth. Julia could see it there, and her pendant in its evidence bag beside it.

"All right. One hand only. Slowly."

Donaldson complied. When he had the phone out he tapped on the face to turn on the recorder and set it carefully on the arm of his chair.

"This is Detective Manfred Donaldson," he said, "conducting a voluntary interview with Harriet Miller in her home. Please state your name and that this statement is given voluntarily."

"This is Harriet Miller," she said. "I'm holding Mister Donaldson at gunpoint. No one is making me say or do anything. Will that do?"

"That ought to cover it," he agreed drily. "Go ahead."

"Okay. We moved here to Oregon in '79 and the first spring we were here Charlie noticed that there's a meadow down the hill that's especially good for growing morel mushrooms. You know the ones I mean, Detective? Little tan things, look like sponges, shaped kind of like Christmas trees."

"I know what they are. They're fairly common, as far as I know."

"They are. And there are tricks you can use to get more of them to grow. Collect them in a mesh bag is one. Everybody knows that. When you're walking around the woods with a mesh bag of morels the spores shake out and if you retrace your steps the next day you find more mushrooms. Charlie took it further, though. He'd make a slurry of manure and water, a little peat moss and some ground up mushrooms and he'd spread it around the meadow. Splash it around where there was shade and deadwood. Every year he'd get a bumper crop. It was nothing sinister. He just liked mushrooms. We'd eat our fill and sell the rest in the parking lot down at the convenience store on the corner. They'd bring in four or five dollars a pound and we could always use the money."

"Okay," Donaldson said, "but that isn't a motive for murder. What happened?"

"It was 1986," Harriet said. "Chernobyl happened."

"Chern-- The nuclear reactor? In Russia? How the hell does something that happened in Russia--"

"It blew up," Harriet emphasized every word. "In the spring of 1986, it blew up and when it did it wiped out the east Asian mushroom fields. Overnight the price of mushrooms skyrocketed. They went from four or five dollars a pound to twenty dollars a pound. That was a fortune then. When Julia saw Charlie in the woods, he was carrying about $1,000 worth of mushrooms. And that was just from one day's work."

"So you killed her because...you were afraid she was going to steal your mushrooms?"

"No." Harriet was disgusted. "We were *afraid* she was going to talk about them."

"Okay, now I really don't understand."

"Y'know, it seemed like a godsend," she said. "Charlie was sick with cancer for the first time then. He was getting treated at the VA but they barely covered the medicines. The chemo was making him so sick. He couldn't eat, couldn't sleep, he certainly couldn't work. I tried to take up the slack. I was working down at the store when they could give me hours, cleaning houses, babysitting, and trying to take care of him all at the same time. We were barely bringing in enough to put food on the table and feed our animals. All our bills were getting behind. And then, all of a sudden, Charlie's mushrooms, of all things, were worth a fortune."

"But what happened?"

"The pickers came. Asians, a lot of them. Day laborers. They followed the mushroom crops, working their way up the coast from California. There was a law, you see. You could only take so many mushrooms per person from public lands each day. Not very many. Four or five, maybe? But if you bought a day license for a dollar, you could take as many as you could find. So they'd buy their licenses and pick mushrooms all day. They had camps set up to sleep at night. There was a big one on the road to Corvallis. We'd drive past it every time I had to take Charlie to the VA.

"Charlie already told you, he went to Vietnam. He was captured and held in a P.O.W. camp. Every time we'd drive by the pickers' camps he'd have flashbacks and nightmares. And he was already so sick."

"So...you killed Julia Lodge because you were afraid the Asians were going to steal your mushrooms?" Donaldson said uncertainly.

"We were afraid they were going to find out about the meadow, how fertile it was and how many mushrooms we were getting."

"But that's nonsense. All you would have had to do was call the police and report them for trespassing."

"We couldn't," Harriet said, "*because we didn't own our property then.*"

"I'm sorry. You what?"

"We didn't own this property. We were squatting here. We met in California, after Charlie came home from Vietnam. He was lost, disillusioned. Drifted from job to job, couldn't seem to settle or make anything stick. He got involved with the peace movement and advocating for MIAs and POWs who were still unaccounted for. I was a widow. Richard, my first husband, had been killed in a car accident. He'd been a veterinarian. I was his nurse. I worked for another vet for a while, but I had Rick's equipment and I'd also take care of animals people brought me. Like I still do here. I met Charlie when he brought me a dog someone had shot with a BB gun and we hit it off.

"We made our way up the coast. Running away from our pasts and trying to find a place to make a new life. This farm was abandoned when we found it. The last owner had died and didn't have any heirs. So we just moved in and fixed it up. Paid the taxes to keep it from going to auction until we could afford to buy it ourselves. If the mushroom pickers found out we didn't own the place, they could have had us thrown out. We'd have lost everything, and Charlie was so sick."

"You couldn't have just asked me not to say anything?" Julia demanded.

"You couldn't have just asked her to keep her mouth shut?" Donaldson asked, as if he'd heard her.

"I may not have used the best judgement," Harriet allowed.

"You think?" Donaldson shook his head. "Tell me about Julia. How did she die?"

"Painlessly. I'm not a monster. And I do know how to put something down gently. That's something every vet needs to know."

"Stop saying that," Julia shouted. "I wasn't a wounded animal. You didn't 'put me down'. I was a human being and you murdered me."

"She was down in the beach house, asleep in the big bedroom with her little boy."

"It was a dark night," Donaldson said. "You took the footpath in front of your house down to the beach and walked across the sand. Your steps stirred up the micro-organisms and left a blue glow in your wake."

"Yes, that's right," she said. "How did you know that?"

"Jude Lodge saw you. He woke up and looked out the window and saw the light you stirred up. He thought it was pretty. He didn't know it meant you were coming to kill his mother."

"They were sleeping with the window open. I soaked a cloth with chloroform and reached in and put it on the pillow. Then I waited for it to take effect. In the movies they just wave a little chloroform under someone's nose and they collapse, but it doesn't work like that in the real world. I gave them about twenty minutes. By the time I went in they were both sound asleep."

"That's why Jude was sick to the stomach the next morning," Donaldson said. "Because he'd been drugged."

"Yes, probably. Poor little tyke. I didn't intend for that to happen."

"You're crazy," Julia said, looming over the other woman. "You know that, right? You're absolutely fucking insane."

"And when you killed Julia," Donaldson said, "you used the same thing you used on the deer, didn't you? The knacker gun? And you used her pillows to muffle the sound, but it still made some noise, like a screen door slamming?"

"Yes. But I used it at the base of her spine, so it would crush the nerve bundle there. I wanted to make sure she didn't feel anything. I pulled her off the side of the bed and opened her throat and bled her out into a 5-gallon bucket. Then I emptied it into the sea."

"But you got some blood on Julia's pillows. When Jude woke up the next morning he smelled something that he said smelled like burning hair. He decided later that it must have been pot, but it wasn't, was it? You were burning Julia's feather pillows."

"Oh, that's right," Harriet said in wonder. "I meant to replace them with two of ours. I guess I forgot. All these years, I never remembered that." She shook herself. "Oh, well. It hardly matters now. Did you have any other questions, Mister Donaldson?"

"You know," he said carefully, watching the barrel of her gun, "even though I never read you your rights, the fact that you've given this statement voluntarily means we are going to be able to use it against you in a court of law."

"Oh, I don't think so." She stroked Charlie's hand and arm affectionately.

He was still now, his chest barely moving. Julia, looking not just at him but inside him, saw a small pool of light still gathered in his chest, threading its way up to the increasingly detailed form floating above.

"Everything I did," Harriet said, "I did for Charlie. I regret that it had to happen, but not that I did it. I love him. And I've known all along that I couldn't live without him. That's why I made arrangements for Jasmine to take the dog, you see."

Even as Donaldson tensed and poised himself for action, Harriet swung the muzzle of the gun around and pointed it at her own temple. But Julia was close and she was faster.

She saw it all as if time were standing still for her. Donaldson half out of his seat, with his hands on the chair arms and his phone in midair, falling to the floor. Charlie's astral form beginning to twitch like a newborn fawn. Harriet's finger tightening on the trigger. The room sang with emotion and Julia took it all, drew it all in and focused it on her hand.

She reached into the gun, behind the barrel and above the trigger, and closed her fingers around a tiny metal rod nestled inside a coiled spring. She pulled it out through the body of the weapon. As it cleared the metal, she lost hold on it.

Time sped up again. The trigger clicked. The hammer fell. Donaldson and Harriet both flinched. And, in the silence that roared in to take the place of a gunshot that never sounded, Julia could just hear the faint, metallic *ting* of the firing pin striking the wooden floorboards and bouncing away into the shadows under the bed.

Harriet, stupefied, stared at her weapon until Donaldson pulled it out of her hands. He clicked on the safety, and tossed it over onto the seat of his chair. Then he wrestled her around, face-down on the bed with her eyes turned towards her husband's still body. He cuffed her hands ungently behind her and said, "You're under arrest for the murder of Julia Lodge."

Epilogue

The Power Of Love

[Huey Lewis, 1985]

Funeral parlors always seemed to be in old houses. Perhaps it was a throwback to the days when people laid out their dead at home. Julia's funeral was being held at Gunderson and Strahm Funeral Home, a big white house with black trim and a deep verandah. It sat, with it's manicured lawn and carefully-trimmed shrubbery, incongruous in the middle of a business district in northwest Portland. Julia, following Donaldson through the building and into the Orchid room, had to pause to read her own name on the placard outside.

Julia Ann Meyers Lodge, it read in elegant script. *Visitation at 1:00 P.M. Service at 3:00.*

An arched double doorway led to a pair of interconnected rooms. The main room held a refreshment table at one end and rows of folding chairs facing Julia's coffin at the other. Her family had chosen a simple casket in polished mahogany. It rested on trestles at the head of the room, closed, surrounded by floral arrangements. The room was filled with pictures of Julia's life, on strategically-placed tables and on the lid of the coffin itself. She saw her wedding picture and graduation pictures from high school and college. Here she was a three-year-old riding a tricycle down the sidewalk and there she sat exhausted in a hospital bed, holding a newborn Jude with John's arms wrapped around both of them.

A smaller room sat at a right angle to the head of the main room. It held more rows of chairs, roped off with a velvet rope. A small plaque on the wall beside it read "family--private."

John and Jude were already there, with Jude's wife and daughters and a scattering of people Julia didn't know, or at least didn't recognize. Karen Lodge--her daughter-in-law--was a large Black woman with a gentle face and a soft voice. She saw Donaldson first, headed towards John, and she nudged Jude and moved to intercept.

"Is there something we can help you with, Detective?"

He barely acknowledged her, keeping his gaze on John as he spoke. "I've just come to pay my respects," he said, his voice formal and carefully neutral.

John heard him. Looked up and came over to join them. "Detective."

"I'm sorry for your loss," Donaldson said as if he had rehearsed it. There was nothing in his tone that suggested he meant the words, but Julia supposed it was worth something that he was even saying them.

"Thank you," John said politely. "And thank you for finding out what happened to her. I know we've had our differences, but I do appreciate your diligence."

"If you'd been open with me we might have reached this conclusion years ago," Donaldson replied. His formality slipped and a trace of resentment bled through.

John just nodded slightly. "You're right. I'm sorry."

Jude had come up behind his father on his right even as Karen fell back behind his left shoulder, so that the two were flanking him and buttressing him. Jude put a hand on the back of John's neck and squeezed lightly.

"What's going to happen to Harriet Miller?" he asked.

Donaldson sighed. "For the time being she's undergoing a psychiatric evaluation. Given her age, it's likely she'll spend the rest of her life institutionalized. If she is ever released, she'll probably be transferred to prison. That will be for a judge to decide, though. I've concluded the investigation and turned over the evidence to the district attorney. What happens now is out of my hands."

"What about her gun?" John asked. "Did they figure out why it didn't fire?"

Donaldson shoved his hands down in his pockets,

208

looked at the floor and shuffled his feet. "The firing pin had come out. They found it on the floor in the corner."

"But I thought she'd already fired it once. How could it come out without the gun being disassembled? Is that even possible?"

"It shouldn't be."

"But then...?"

Donaldson sighed deeply. "I'm not endorsing this explanation. I just want to be clear on that. But Charlie was practically dead at that point, even if he was still barely breathing. It has been suggested that his spirit somehow interceded on her behalf."

"Do you believe that?" Jude demanded.

"I don't believe anything. I'm just telling you the closest thing to an explanation that anyone has come up with so far."

"Give him the necklace," Julia said, coming up right behind Donaldson and speaking in his ear. "Give him the necklace. Give him the necklace. Give John my necklace."

Donaldson dipped a hand in his coat pocket and came up with the evidence bag with the pendant sealed inside.

"This was found with your wife's body," he said. "We were keeping it for evidence, but since Harriet Miller has confessed there won't be a trial. I thought that you should have it."

He handed it over and John took it reverently. His hands were shaking and Julia saw that his palms and fingertips were rough and callused. His knuckles were swollen with arthritis and the veins stood out blue on the back of his hand.

"Look, Jude. Your mother's necklace. Do you remember this?" He showed it to Jude and then to Karen. "Jude found the stone on the beach the summer before." He didn't have to specify before what. They all knew. "I had the three J's engraved on it, for John, Jude, and Julia, and a hole drilled. We put it on a chain and gave it to her that last Christmas. I don't believe she ever took it off."

"What a sweet memory," Karen said. "We should get another chain and you can wear it now."

"I'd like that," John agreed, "for a while. Someday I'd like to pass it on to little Julia." Julia's namesake was a sprightly child of about seven, with her mother's eyes and her grand-mother's nose and just a little something of John about her mouth. Her little sister, Lily, was a feminine version of Jude that last summer, when he was four. They were seated on folding chairs in the back of the viewing area, pretty in black dresses, whispering back and forth and watching the proceedings with big, dark eyes.

"It's not fair," Jude said bitterly. "It's just not god-damned fair. That woman *killed* my mother, but she gets saved by a miraculous intervention? Where was Mom's miracle? Why should Harriet Miller get to live but Mom didn't? It's not fair!"

Julia stood close to him, hoping her son could feel her presence. A tendril of soft hair had fallen across his eyes and she tried to brush it back with her fingers, standing on tiptoe to place a gentle kiss on his temple.

"Oh, sweetheart. Harriet thinks she can't live without Charlie," she said. Her voice turned hard. "But you and your father had to live without me."

"Well," Donaldson said uncomfortably, "I should be go-ing. Again, my condolences."

"Thank you." John offered his hand and after a slight hesitation Donaldson shook it. Then he turned and strode off the way he had come.

Julia had become accustomed to following him and she did again, as far as the double doors, relishing the prospect of watching him walk away. It was a strange sensation, to know that you would miss someone in spite of yourself and to simul-taneously hope you never saw them again.

At the door he met Min, dressed in civilian clothes and carrying a calla lily plant. His gaze raked up and down her figure and when he opened his mouth to speak, she visibly braced herself.

"You look," he froze and seemed to be fishing for a word. "Nice," he said, finally, delivering the compliment defensively, almost belligerently. "Is that good? Is that okay? Okay, fine. You look nice already." He spun away and stomped down the hall muttering to himself, his palms turned up, leaving two women, one living and solid and one ethereal, staring after him.

"What in the holy hell was that all about?" Min demanded.

"I think he's trying not to be an asshole," Julia said in wonderment.

Min shrugged and took her plant on into the room, but Julia lingered. She could feel something important about to happen. Someone was coming, a turbulent storm of emotion that jangled her sensibilities like a wind in the wires of a sailing ship.

Shadows fell across the frosted light in the main door. It opened and Rose Meyer came in, a slash of bright sunlight preceding her.

She was dressed all in black, a pretty, knee-length dress with dark hose and sensible black shoes. Her hair was twisted up in a severe bun and she carried a little handbag that she clutched in front of her in both hands. Julia's Aunt Marjorie was with her, her hair white now but looking otherwise unchanged, and they were accompanied by two younger women Julia didn't know. Annie, maybe, and Baby Cindy all grown up?

Rose marched down the hall, her heels clacking on the hardwood floor, and headed for John. Julia longed to get between them, as she had in life, but she was insubstantial here. She had no agency to alter whatever was about to happen, nor to do anything but watch it unfold.

"You should have come to me," Rose said without preamble. "I would have helped you. I would have helped Belle. We were family. You owed me that."

For the second time in less than ten minutes John was met with harsh criticism and for the second time he did not defend himself but lowered his head, closed his eyes and agreed.

"Yes, I know. You're right. I'm sorry."

"Grandma--" Jude tried to intercede but Marjorie put an arm around him and led him away.

"Let them talk. They need to talk."

"Still," Rose said, "I owe you an apology. I've always known Julia had good judgement. I shouldn't have doubted her judgement in you. I should have seen everything that you were struggling with and I shouldn't have pushed you away. And I should have never believed the worst of you. But," her shoulders and her voice trembled. Tears, at long last, spilled down her cheeks. The words had gone unspoken for so long they'd hardened to stone in her mouth. She forced them out now, one at a time. "She was my baby."

John was weeping too, but he put a gentle hand below her chin and drew her face up so he could meet her gaze.

"I understand," he said. "I have a son."

He opened his arms and she stepped into his embrace. Julia felt a sudden lightness of spirit, a release from a weight she hadn't been aware she was carrying.

"There's a strange sort of symmetry to it," Karen offered. "Julia died when she wanted to live. Harriet lived when she wanted to die."

"God will prevail in all things," Marjorie counseled sagely. "Take care of your family and trust in God."

"I don't know about that," Julia said, "though I suppose there's a good chance I'm about to find out." She knew, without knowing how she knew, that her time among them was coming to an end. She focused on Jude. "It's time for me to go now, sweetheart. I can't do anything more staying here. I'll see you someday on the other side. Live a good life. Take care of your father for me, and your wife and those beautiful little girls, and remember Momma loves you."

She put her arms around him and kissed him softly on the cheek, hoping that somehow he would sense her presence. She hated to leave him, to leave any of them, but she could feel something indefinable pulling her away.

She said goodbye to Marjorie and to her mother. Rose was in her eighties now and a simple understanding of average life spans told her that it wouldn't be too many years before they were together again. Still it was hard to say farewell.

Leaving John was the hardest parting of all.

He was standing alone beside her coffin, studying their wedding picture. She stopped in front of him and stared into his eyes. He was still in there. Beyond the years, under the wrinkles and white hair, behind all the sorrows, he was still John.

"I'll be waiting," she said, "when your journey's over." She leaned in and placed her lips against his and it felt so *real*, as if she were really flesh touching flesh, his lungs breathing life into her body. She didn't know if the tears she tasted were his or her own.

"I was not wrong to love you," she whispered and then, because she had to, she turned away.

The light was in the hallway. She could see it, moving across the walls like a living thing and maybe it was. Again she was reminded of the glass heart and a thousand memories connected with that. She went in search of it and found Charlie sitting on a wicker bench waiting for her. His astral body looked young still, but his eyes were old. Even if she hadn't seen him dying, she'd have recognized him.

She stopped in the doorway and looked him in the eye. He reddened and swallowed but didn't look away.

"I know it's no use saying I'm sorry," he said, "but I am."

"I'm not sure how I feel about you right now," she told him. "What Harry did to me, killing me like that, that wasn't your fault, you know? No more than it was Belle's fault that she was raped or John's fault that he wasn't there that night. And you refused to help her frame John when it would have made things easier for you. I respect that.

"But my family spent more than thirty years wondering what happened to me. It tore them apart. Jude had to grow up with that uncertainty. John lived all those years under suspicion and he was innocent. You could have spared them that."

"You're right. I know. And I got no defense for that. I should have done the right thing and told what I knew. But I couldn't. I couldn't betray my wife. Because she did it for me. And she was all I had. She was all I ever had."'

Julia thought it over but she had no response. For good or for bad, she wasn't ready to offer him absolution. "So what happens now?" she asked finally.

He stood and put his hands in his pockets. "When I was dying, those last few days when I couldn't get up and it was just a matter of time, I started seeing people. My mom, my granddad. Even my old dog Blue was in the room for a while. They all told me everything'll be okay and to go into the light, but I ain't prepared to do that yet."

"Oh?"

"No, ma'am." He shuffled his feet. "I'm gonna wait around for Harriet. We did a wrong thing and I ain't sure where we're gonna end up. And that scares me, to be truthful, more'n I can say. But it don't matter. Wherever we go, we're going together. But first I have a promise to keep."

She nodded for him to continue.

"I didn't just see people I knew," he said. "There was a man there I didn't recognize. A big Black man in an old green sweater with an ink stain on the pocket."

"My dad," she said. "You described my dad. Mom wanted to throw that sweater out but he wouldn't let her. He loved that thing. We buried him in it. That was my dad."

"Yes, ma'am. He said as much. He said you got lost. He's been trying to reach you but you couldn't see him. He needed someone who hadn't crossed over yet to find you and bring you into the light. I promised him I would and here I am. I brought you the light so you can go home."

Julia gazed into the glow. It was beautiful but she couldn't see anything beyond. "Really?" she breathed. "Really?"

"Really. Oh, and I'm supposed to tell you something."

She glanced at him.

"He said he still has your necklace. He'll give it back when he sees you again."

Julia took a look behind her. The main room was beginning to fill with people, mostly strangers to her. She wanted to see her family one last time but the angle was wrong and the light pulled at her. She turned again to Charlie.

"Your life was hard," she said. "I know it was. And I'm still not sure I'm ready to forgive you, but I do hope you find peace someday."

"Thank you."

She put one hand tentatively into the light and froze as a new sound reached her ears.

"Do you hear that?" she asked in wonder. "Oh! Do you hear that?"

"I don't hear anything. What is it?"

"It's Belle! My sister-in-law. She's singing Madonna!"

Charlie frowned, uncertain. "What, you mean like...Ave Maria?"

Julia favored him with a brilliant smile. "No. Material Girl."

Within the light a hand, warm and solid and real, closed over her own. With it came a sense of peace and love and safety. Julia turned her back on the world. She squared her shoulders, took a deep breath, and, at long last, stepped out of death and into eternity.

Acknowledgments

No book is written in a vacuum. This book, though, is probably unique in that many of the people who helped me had no idea they were doing so.

When I first conceived the plot for this book I was hesitant about writing it. Julia Lodge is a Black woman and I (as has been pointed out to me) am not. I felt inadequate to take on such a project. I persisted because I feel strongly that representation matters and there is not enough diversity in mystery publishing. The ideal, of course, is to open up opportunities for Black authors (and other marginalized people) to tell their own stories in their own words. But I believe that it's also incumbent upon me, as a white writer, to be more inclusive in my own work.

While working on this book I have been blessed with a plethora of Black Twitter friends, who have shared their lives, memories, fears, hopes, opinions, and occasional weirdness with the world. I have learned more by listening to them than I can say and I am eternally grateful.

I'd like to thank my friend, award- winning author Kellye Garrett (yes, I'm name-dropping) for her wise counsel. Kellye leads a group called Crime Writers of Color, to support and promote minority authors and help them find space to tell their own stories in their own voices. You can find them on Twitter at #cwoc.

Helen Kelley Burroughs is an editor and sensitivity read-er whose work on this was invaluable.

This gorgeous cover design is by Robin Monde Locke. I can't say enough about how much I love her work.

Finally, a huge, huge, MASSIVE thank you to my friend and fellow writer, Bill Cameron. (Yes, still name-dropping.) Bill is an Oregon-based mystery writer, active in the left coast writing community, who also speaks about writing and publishing and conducts workshops. He is familiar with the locations in this book and was beyond generous with his time and energy in helping me and answering my questions.

(Any errors, of course, are entirely on me. Also, I rearranged the coast around Waldport—I do hope no one minds.)

About the Author

Loretta Ross is a mystery writer and crazy cat lady who lives in rural Missouri. She's an alumna of Cottey College and has a BA in art history and archeology from the University of Missouri at Columbia. An avid Kansas City Royals baseball fan, she has a lifelong interest in true ghost stories, reincarnation, and history. A natural introvert, Loretta was social distancing before it was cool. She's spent the pandemic binge-watching archeology documentaries and YouTube videos and serving as overstuffed furniture for various feline members of the family.

You can pry her Oxford comma from her cold, dead, sentence structure.